PUBLISHE

This is the sixth volume of Charlie Small's journal and you'll never guess how it came to light! A weather-beaten North Sea fisherman turned up at our office one day, dressed in sou'wester and waders!

'Thought you might be interested in this,' he said in a gravelly voice. 'Found it inside a thirty-pound codfish I was a-guttin' for the crew's supper! You won't believe the adventures written in there!' And he placed a scruffy, slime-encrusted Charlie Small journal on our desk.

We thanked the old salt and excitedly read the whole book from cover to cover. The fisherman was right: it's the most amazing, exciting and incredible Charlie Small journal so far. Now, here it is – just for you!

There must be other notebooks to find, so keep your eyes peeled. If you do come across a curious-looking diary, or see a boy who is an expert with a lasso or a snow bazooka, please contact us via the Charlie Small website: www.charliesmall.co.uk.

Who is the mysterious hooded figure?

THE AMAZING ADVENTURES OF CHARLIE SMALL (400)

Notebook -6-

FROSTBITE PASS

Brrr!

Aaargh!
Watch out!

Look out —
old slimy's about!

CHARLIE SMALL JOURNAL 6: FROSTBITE PASS
A RED FOX BOOK 978 1 782 95325 8

First published in Great Britain by David Fickling Books,
previously an imprint of Random House Children's Publishers UK
A Penguin Random House Company

Penguin
Random House
UK

First published as *The Barbarous Brigands of Frostbite Pass* 2008
This Red Fox edition published 2014

3 5 7 9 10 8 6 4

Text and illustrations copyright © Charlie Small, 2008

**Penguin Random House is committed to a sustainable future for
our business, our readers and our planet. This book is made from
Forest Stewardship Council® certified paper.**

MIX
Paper from
responsible sources
FSC® C018179

Printed and bound in Great Britain by Clays Ltd, St Ives plc

Set in 15/17pt Garamond MT

Red Fox Books are published by Random House Children's Publishers UK,
61–63 Uxbridge Road, London W5 5SA

www.**randomhousechildrens**.co.uk
www.**totallyrandombooks**.co.uk
www.**randomhouse**.co.uk

Addresses for companies within The Random House Group Limited can be found at:
www.**randomhouse**.co.uk/offices.htm

THE RANDOM HOUSE GROUP Limited Reg. No. 954009

A CIP catalogue record for this book is available from the British Library.

NAME: Charlie Small

ADDRESS: Somewhere in the Frozen North

AGE: 400 – yes I am!

MOBILE: 07713 12

SCHOOL: Good old St Beckham's Although I didn't think it was that great when I had to go there every day!

THINGS I LIKE: Gorillas; cutlass fighting; Braemar; Jenny and Granny Green; Tom, Eliza and Ma Baldwin

THINGS I HATE: The Puppet Master (a big bully); Joseph Craik (an evil schemer and my arch enemy); scruffers; endless tunnels; the Spidion

If you find this book, **PLEASE** look after it. This is the only true account of my remarkable adventures.

My name is Charlie Small and I am four hundred years old, maybe even more. But in all those long years I have never grown up. Something happened when I was eight years old, something I can't begin to understand. I went on a journey... and I'm still trying to find my way home. Now, although I've been nearly swallowed by a slime monster, attacked by terrible trufflers and befriended by a tribe of weird tree people, I still look like any eight-year-old boy you might pass in the street.

I've travelled to the ends of the earth and to the centre of the earth. I've been robbed by a band of brigands, and have ridden across the night sky on the back of a bad-tempered owl. You may think this sounds fantastic, you could think it's a lie. But you would be wrong, because **EVERYTHING IN THIS BOOK IS TRUE.** Believe this single fact and you can share the most incredible journey ever experienced.

Charlie Small

The Slavering Slime Monster!

Attack Of The Slime Monster

I'm hiding in the tangled roots of a mangrove tree, stranded in a vast, stinking swamp that is home to some of the scariest monsters I have ever seen. Thick green water stretches out in every direction, dotted with hundreds of verdant, jewel-like islands. This is my first night since escaping from the Underworld, and I'm beginning to wish I'd stayed there!

My problems started as soon as I dropped from the sky with my homemade parachute and landed on the shore of a small island. Swamp water boiled and popped all around me; then, all of a sudden, something started to break through the gloopy surface of the bog . . .

A large pointed ear appeared, dripping with gunge; then a pair of sulphurous yellow eyes, flashing with a malevolent light.

'Yikes!' I cried and tried to run, but my legs wouldn't work. I was frozen with fear. Now a warty nose appeared and gaping jaws, gurgling in a ferocious roar. *Jeepers creepers!* I thought. *It's some sort of slime monster!*

The monster continued to rise up out of the swamp until it towered above me, standing waist deep in the bubbling bog. It was huge and covered in long olive-green fur. As it roared, it showed a set of slab-like teeth as big as gravestones. At last I managed to break into a run; but it was already too late! The monster reached out a hairy arm and grabbed hold of me.

I felt giant claws close around me. Now I know what it's like to be a car in one of those automatic washers! I struggled and writhed, desperate to escape, and as the creature tried to grip me even tighter, I shot from its slimy paw like a bar of wet soap in a bubble bath!

Yikes! I flew through the air, turning somersaults and cartwheels, and landed in a heap on a soft bed of ferns. I scrambled to my feet, but my freedom didn't last

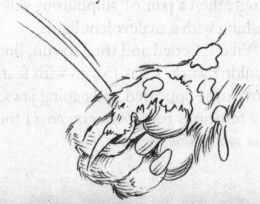

long. The monster reached over and grabbed me again. Once more I was squirted from its slippery grip.

'Gnar!' It roared in frustration as I tried to scramble to safety. But there was nowhere to hide. The only cover on the island was the bank of feathery ferns where I'd landed, and one tiny tree. In desperation I crouched behind the narrow trunk but the slime monster spotted me and, stretching out an arm, ripped the tree out by its roots. *Jeepers!* I thought. That was as easy as picking a daisy.

'Gnash!' the monster bellowed. Then, wiping a paw dry on the ground, it snatched me up and in one swift movement popped me into its mouth!

Charlie Small On The Menu!

I landed on the slime monster's damp, spongy tongue and bounced as if I had just taken a running jump onto my bed. Then, *Whoa!* I started to slip and, just like being on a super-splash slide at a swimming pool, went speeding towards the giant, grinding teeth.

'Help!' I cried. 'Let me out of here, you great greasy goon!'

Its teeth crashed together, missing my head by millimetres. The monster tried to push me between them with its slobbery tongue. I dived down, sliding and bouncing against its tonsils. I just managed to avoid dropping down the monster's throat by grabbing hold of a jagged molar! I had to do something fast, or I would be crushed to a pulp between the enormous hammering gnashers!

I sat up, covered in saliva, and as the monster rolled its tongue, I went scooting back towards its teeth. I opened the flap of my rucksack, searching for the one thing that might do the trick: the sandwiches that Ma Baldwin had given me before I escaped from the Underworld!

I knew, just by the smell, what was in the sarnies as soon as she handed me the parcel: my least favourite food in the entire Underworld. It was Ma's own concoction – a dark, strong and eye-wateringly sour spread that I called Ma-mite! Perhaps the slime monster would feel the same way as I did about it. As I slid, spinning and spiralling in a pool of spit, towards the chewing chompers, I ripped open the sandwiches and smeared a big streak of the filling over the monster's tongue!

It stopped chewing almost immediately, swallowed (nearly sending me careering down into its stomach) and then spat as hard as it could!

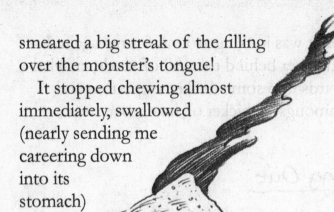

'Ptah! Yee-uk!' yelled the slime monster as I went flying out between its rubbery lips in a spray of saliva. I sailed right over the island, across a stretch of green swamp water, and landed in the shallows next to another, bigger island. I climbed up the bank and crouched between some reeds, looking back as the monster cupped its paws and took a big swig of water, gargling and spitting out the taste of Ma-mite.

Then it was looking around for me again. I ducked lower behind the wall of reeds, crawled backwards into some thicker vegetation and crept amongst a thicket of mangrove trees.

Hiding Out

For the best part of an hour the growling slime monster waded up and down through the swamp looking for me. It went from island to island, raking its claws through the reeds and ferns. It lifted its warty snout in the air and sniffed, trying to pick up my scent. It put a great yellow eye up against the very tree I was hiding in, trying to see into the dark tangle of

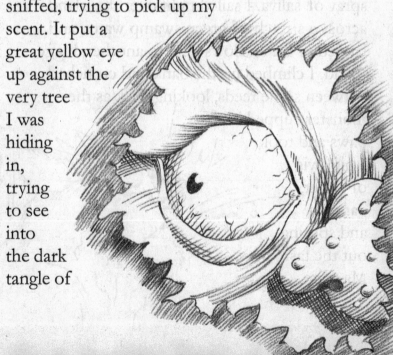

branches. I lay very still, hardly daring to breathe as the eye swivelled this way and that, the stinky breath making the leaves flutter all around me.

Then, suddenly, the monster seemed to give up, turned on its heel and waded off through the swamp. I heaved a huge sigh of relief – and the monster's ears twitched. *No, you fool, Charlie – won't you ever learn to keep quiet?* The creature came storming back, grabbed a handful of trees, and pulled and tugged, tearing them up from the soil. Grunting with frustration, it shook the trees, sending a shower of mud and stones into the swamp. Then, finding nothing, it roared in disappointment and went to grab another handful; a handful that would include me! But just as it reached out, the swamp water nearby exploded in a cascade of bubbles and an arrow-shaped head, followed by a long thick neck, snaked out of the water . . .

A Mighty Battle

At first I thought it *was* a snake, but then I saw its little front arms and the scaly fins fanning out from its jaw. As the creature let out a long,

9

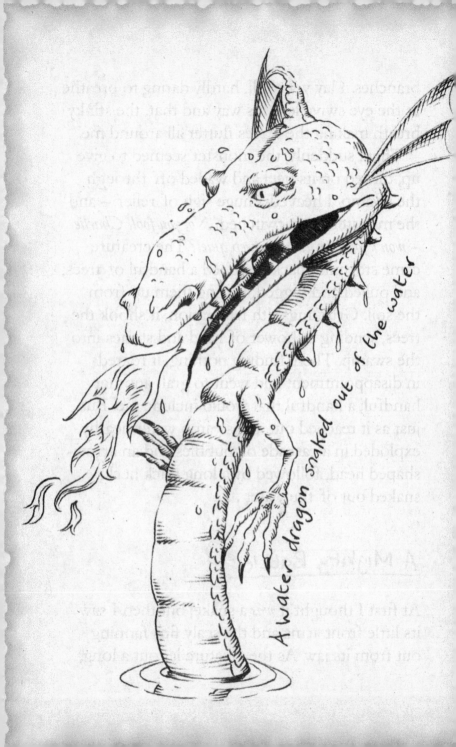

A water dragon snaked out of the water

threatening hiss, I saw a red tapering tongue of flame flick from its mouth, singeing the slime monster's fur, and I realized this must be some sort of water dragon. The monster lunged forward and grabbed the dragon by the snout, forcing its head back. The dragon's scaly tail whipped out of the swamp and wrapped itself around the monster's hairy neck, squeezing tightly and making it croak and gasp for air.

With a titanic effort, the slime monster pulled at the scaly tail, forcing it away and gradually unwinding it. Then it took a huge lungful of air before launching a right hook that caught the water dragon under the jaw. '*Aarrk!*' screamed the reptile, and spat out a broken tooth. (Darn it – the tooth fell into the swamp. I would have loved to add that to my collection!)

I watched spellbound as the mighty combatants toppled into the mire with an enormous splash, wrestling and roaring, grappling and struggling. First the punching, thumping slime monster seemed to be winning the fight; then the snapping water dragon shot out a ball of fire, forcing the monster to retreat and douse his smoking fur with swamp water. The slime monster charged and, leaping onto its enemy, clutched it around the throat with both its huge paws. The water dragon gasped, sending a puff of black smoke into the air. It seemed to be all over for the formidable flame-thrower. Then, with an enormous roar, it flexed its long muscly neck and broke free of the slime monster's grasp.

Stepping back, the water dragon snarled, arched its neck and opened its slender jaws. A plume of roaring flame filled the air. The slime monster backed away, growling and holding up its paws to shield itself from the heat. Then the two antagonists stood staring at each other, swaying to left and right, looking for a chance to attack.

All of a sudden, as if in mutual agreement, and with plenty of grunts and barks, the beasts started backing away until, finally, the dragon dipped its head under the surface of the water and swam off without a ripple. The slime monster stood up to its middle in the bog, its head bowed and its chest heaving with exhaustion; then it too slowly waded away. I was left on my own in the silence of the swamp.

Bedtime zzzz

I waited for a long time in my hiding place in the mangrove tree. Finally I felt it was safe to come out. Then, creeping down to the water's edge, still shaking slightly from the fear and excitement of having watched two mythical monsters battle it out in front of my eyes, I looked out across the swamp. The water was as flat as a tabletop, with only the occasional bubble popping to the surface. The monsters had gone, and as the big orange sun was starting to set in the sky, I decided it was time to find somewhere safe to spend the night.

Back in the middle of the grove of trees, I looked around for a likely sleeping place. I didn't fancy kipping up in the branches, just in case old slimy came back again, and I certainly didn't want to curl up on the ground – *Yeurgh!* Who knows what would slither over me during the night! Then I spotted the perfect place.

All the mangrove trees seemed to be standing on tiptoe, their intertwined roots growing above ground as if they were on stilts! Some of the root systems had grown into a cone, making a sort of natural tepee, so, choosing one of the largest trees, I forced the outer roots apart and climbed inside, just like this:

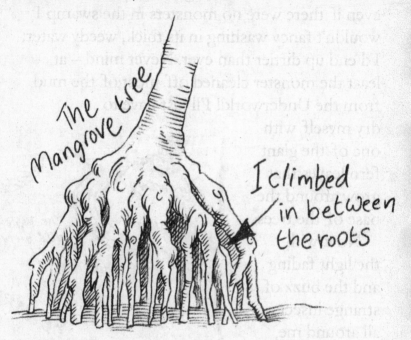

The Mangrove tree

I climbed in between the roots

Fantastic! Inside it was dry and quite warm, just like being in a tent. The roots were woven so closely together that I would be all but invisible from the outside. It was a perfect den.

I spread out my tatty old coat for a mattress and placed my rucksack at one end as a pillow. I took out a few of the lumpier things and then stuffed handfuls of fallen leaves inside to make it as comfortable as possible.

I wish I could have a wash – I'm still covered in the slime monster's disgusting spit! But even if there were no monsters in the swamp I wouldn't fancy washing in its thick, weedy water; I'd end up dirtier than ever. Never mind – at least the monster cleaned off most of the mud from the Underworld! I'll just have to dry myself with one of the giant fern leaves that grow around the base of the trees.

Now, with the light fading and the buzz of strange insects all around me, I've finished writing my journal. Tomorrow I will start my journey to Jakeman's factory, and he can tell me how I can finally get back home. But it's not going to be easy;

My factory

←Village

The Wide Wild River

High Hills

BEWARE!

How to find your way to Jakeman's Factory

I think I might be able to get you home, so make your way to my factory and I will meet you there. Be careful—it's a long and dangerous journey. Good luck and see you soon.

From your pal, William Jakeman
Inventor.

all I have to help me is a map he gave me, with the words *Unknown and probably very dangerous* scrawled across it! Fat lot of good that's going to be! Oh well, I'm sure everything will look better in the morning!

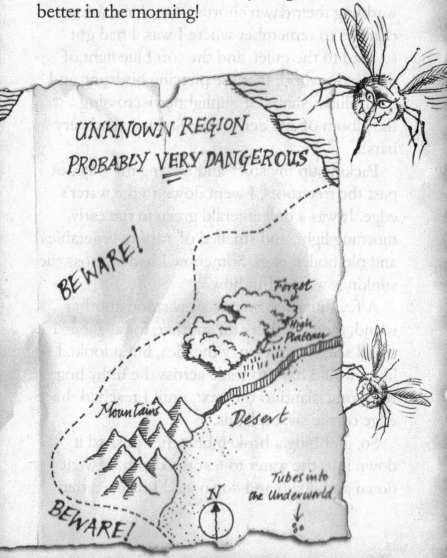

Time To Go Rafting Again

I woke up very early, to the cacophony of a thousand birds tweeting and crowing and warbling their dawn chorus. It took me a few minutes to remember where I was. I had got so used to the quiet, and the soft blue light of the Underworld, that the piercing birdsong and the brilliant shafts of sunlight crisscrossing the gloom of my den seemed strange and very harsh.

Packing up my stuff and forcing my way out past the tree roots, I went down to the water's edge. It was a dull emerald green in the early morning light, and smelled of rotting vegetables and old boiled eggs. Somehow I had to cross the stinking swamp. But how?

A few hundred metres away stood another island, then another and another, for as far as I could see. I didn't fancy the idea, but it looked like I would have to wade across the filthy bog, from one island to the next, until I reached the edge of the swamplands.

So, grabbing a broken branch, I pushed it down into the water to test the depth. It went down and down and down, and I realized that it was far too deep for me to wade in. Not only that, but the water was too gloopy to try and swim through – I would've been sucked down into the swamp before I'd got halfway to the next island! What was I going to do?

There was only one thing for it: if I didn't want to be stranded for ever, I would have to build some sort of boat. Another raft, like the one I started my adventures on four hundred years ago. Brilliant!

I explored my little island for materials, keeping a wary eye on the swamp in case the slime monster or the water dragon decided to come back. The sight of these two beasts battling it out had been awesome. Awesome and scary! I didn't want to have to deal with either of them again. Luckily, though, the swamp now looked peaceful and calm.

There were plenty of raw materials for my raft – when old slimy had pulled up that clump of trees looking for me, loads of branches of different sizes had been shaken loose. I sorted through them, choosing the sturdiest-looking logs, and placed them side by side. Then, using two branches to act as cross-battens for strength, I lashed the whole lot together with the tough strands of vegetation growing in the grove of trees. Soon I'd built a perfect raft, just the way Dad had shown me:

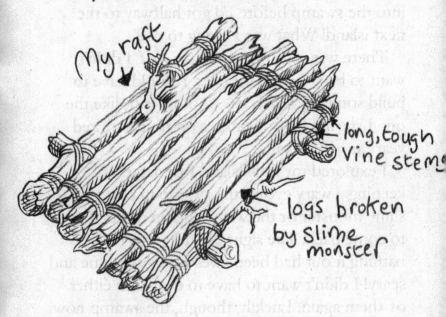

My raft

long, tough vine stems

logs broken by slime monster

Launch Of HMS Charlie Small!

I dragged my raft to the waterside and pushed it in. Guess what? It floated – *Yippee!* Sure, it sat a little lopsidedly, but it definitely floated. Then, sprinkling a handful of water over the raft's bow, I ceremoniously christened it the HMS *Charlie Small*; well, it is probably the only chance I'll ever get to have a boat named after me! Tying the raft to a tree with a bit of string from my explorer's kit, I went to choose a suitable paddle and to see if I could find some food for the voyage.

I was hungry again, but I didn't fancy the soggy remains of Ma's Ma-mite sandwich; perhaps there was some fruit growing on the island? A nice juicy apple would go down a treat. But no such luck – there was plenty of fruit all right, but I didn't recognize any of it: there were festoons of bright red berries with dark blue leaves; sickly green fruit as large as grapefruit; and purple plums with long prickly spikes. Trouble was, how could I tell if they were poisonous or not!

Just then a little animal emerged from the undergrowth and looked around nervously. I held my breath and kept very still as it darted over a grassy hummock towards some bushes. It looked a bit like a squirrel and a bit like a beaver, but was much, much smaller – hardly bigger than a sparrow! It had orange webbed feet like a duck for swimming, big buck-teeth for gnawing, and a long striped tail like a monkey's for climbing. What a weird creature – and obviously another new species to record in my journal. I decided to call it the 'squarrow'. Here's a quick sketch!

Oh, nuts!

This is the little Squarrow I saw

Creeping nervously over the ground, the animal plucked some nuts from the branches and nibbled away. Well, if they were good enough for a squarrow, I thought, they might be all right for me! When the squarrow had finished feeding and disappeared into the undergrowth again, I picked a big pocketful of nuts. I think I will try just one nut first, and then, if I don't get sick, I can eat some more; better to be safe than sorry!

Having chosen a sturdy stick for my paddle, I went back, untied my raft and climbed aboard. I wedged my rucksack safely in the middle to stop it rolling off, then knelt down and pushed against the bank. With a worrying wobble that sent a wave of water flooding around my knees, I floated away from the shore. Digging my paddle into the viscous swamp, I heaved it back and my raft moved sluggishly through the water. The swamp was so gloopy it was difficult to propel myself forwards – it was like paddling through porridge! This wasn't going to be easy . . .

Stuck In The Swamp

The swamp was like a jigsaw of islands – some only separated by a narrow channel, others sitting alone in a wide stretch of brackish water. I paddled along until the sun was high in the sky and my arms were hurting from the effort. Compared to the river back home, this was really hard work! The water was thick with slime and every time I lifted my paddle, great gloops of gunge dripped thickly from the end.

I was starting to get hot under the noonday sun, so I decided to stop for a rest and a bite to eat. I took a mouthful of water from the bottle in my rucksack. It was warm but wonderful – I don't know what I would have done without this vital piece of exploring kit. After testing the nuts, I decided they were perfectly safe to eat and crunched down on a mouthful of them. They tasted like burnt toast, but I didn't mind. Compared to some of the stuff I'd had to eat with my poor subterranean friends down in the Underworld, they tasted delicious!

Strange insects hummed around me in the warm, humid air. They bumped against my face and buzzed into my eyes so I continually had to swat them away. Soon I was so fed up with the little pests, I decided to get moving again. But when I stuck my oar into the swamp and paddled . . . nothing happened. The swamp was so thick

This wing broke off one of the annoying insects →

with weed I had stuck fast. I could move neither forwards nor backwards! *Oh, bloomin' marvellous.* What was I going to do now?

Toad Attack! (yikes!)

Lifting my oar from the water again, I noticed the thick goo was full of ping-pong-ball-sized bubbles, like some sort of monstrous frogspawn. I wiped the oar clean on the edge of my raft and kicked the gloop back into the swamp. *Ugh!* It was disgusting, and as I knelt there wondering what on earth I should do next, I became aware of a croaking noise.

I saw the surface of the swamp move and then a head popped up: a toad's head, but a toad so large and ugly it made me jump! It was the size of a dinner plate, with a wide, scowling mouth and huge, bulging eyes. Another head appeared; then another, and soon I was surrounded by the critters. They started to swim through the slime towards my raft, snapping their wide, turned-down mouths like manic pedal bins. *Snap! Snap! Snap!* As one toad reached the side of my raft, it snapped again, taking

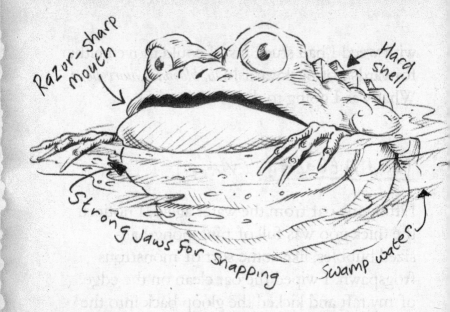

Razor-sharp mouth

Hard shell

Strong jaws for snapping

Swamp water

a huge bite from the log as if it was eating a chocolate flake.

Then they *all* started biting chunks from my raft. *Snip, snap, crack, chomp!* Help! The raft was rapidly disappearing beneath my feet. I swung my paddle at one of the greedy amphibians, but as it swept through the air, the toad lifted its head and caught the oar between its jaws. I desperately tried to pull it back, but the creature's grip was ferocious. With a twist of its head it tore the oar from my grasp. With another bite the oar snapped in two, and I realized I was really up a creek without a paddle!

Now the atrocious toads were hauling

themselves aboard the raft and starting to crawl towards me, their jaws a-snapping. *Yikes!* Pretty soon they would be upon me, and I felt sure that they were going to start snapping at my toes and eating me from the feet up! I had to get off the raft — and fast!

As the weird toads advanced, I noticed they had hard turtle-like shells on their backs, patterned in browns and oranges. They looked like a pack of pernicious paving slabs — and that gave me an idea!

I glanced across the swamp: the water was full of snapping toads, all the way to the steep bank of a small island, and as the leading toad took a first bite at the toe of my trainers, I grabbed my rucksack and launched myself off the raft. Running at full tilt, I raced across the water, using the hard-shelled amphibians as stepping stones. *Yee-hah!* Despite the toads taking a bite out of one of my trainers and removing the lace from the other, I made it. Heart pounding, I leaped onto the island and scrambled up its grassy bank!

I used the toads as stepping stones!

Yee-hah!

I looked back at the swamp – and was shocked and amazed to see the surface boiling with writhing toads as they tore my poor raft to shreds. They were like a shoal of four-legged piranha fish, and I realized that I had only just made it in time. A few seconds later and I would have been stripped to my skeleton!

PREDATOR RATING 18

THE SNAPPING TOAD

The Snapping Toad is a ferocious creature that should be avoided at all costs. It hunts in packs and will attack anything of any size without provocation. With super-strong jaws and a razor-edged mouth, the Snapping Toad is capable of biting through solid steel. Chances of escape are slim! If you are attacked, run like billy-o, but be careful where you place your feet!

WILD ANIMAL COLLECTORS CARDS

Building Bridges!

I jogged over to some trees growing near the bank. They were tall and thin with a sphere of leaves at the top that made them look like lollipops on very long sticks.

Using my mast-climbing pirate skills, I was soon amongst the foliage and pushed the leaves aside to look out over the landscape. *Jeepers creepers!* The swamp went on for ever: small green islands dotted the terrain in every direction, and between them was the interminable sludge of the infernal bog.

'Get me out of here!' I yelled at the top of my voice, and instantly a thousand animal cries filled the air: birds hooted and cawed and cried; hard-shelled frogs croaked and burped; unseen monkeys chattered and screamed – and somewhere something roared!

Whoops! I just *had* to learn to keep my voice down – it's probably not a good idea to advertise your whereabouts if you're surrounded by mythical monsters! Who knows what might be lurking round the next corner.

The next island was about ten metres away. It was much bigger than any others I'd seen, and stretched a long way into the distance. If I could get onto that, I thought, I might find the materials to build a bigger boat, or stumble on another way to get out of the swampland.

The gap between the two islands was much too wide to jump, though, and I wasn't about to try and swim it in case the snapping frogs come after me again. But I had an idea: there *was* a way to get across, if only I could find something in my explorer's kit strong and sharp enough to slice through the tree I was perched in!

I slid down the smooth trunk and opened my rucksack. I heard roars in the distance again. Was it the slime monster? Was it still searching for me? I quickly shuffled through my bag – there must be something that would do the job. Aha! I found just the thing: the enormous serrated megashark's tooth that I'd collected in the Underworld.

(see my Journal The Underworld)

I chose a large stick that was lying on the ground and, using my hunting knife, made a split down one end. Then, wedging the massive tooth in the slit, I bound the end of the stick with some of my explorer's string to hold the tooth tight. Just like this:

Stick

String

My shark-tooth saw

← Very sharp

Brilliant! That should do the trick – a shark-tooth saw. I pulled the tooth backwards and forwards across the bark of the tree trunk – it proved so strong and sharp that it ate through it in no time.

All of a sudden, with a terrible cracking and splintering, the tree started to topple.

'Timber!' I called, and I heard the unknown beast roar once more. *Shut up, you twit*, I told myself, *or else you'll end up as some awful swamp fiend's mid-morning snack!*

The tree crashed to the ground and I raced down to the shore. Fantastic, it worked! The top of the tree had landed amongst the woody reeds on the edge of the big island. Now there was a bridge across the swamp. Grabbing my rucksack, I ran across the narrow trunk.

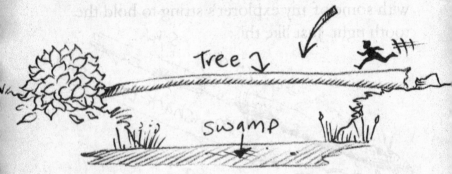

Are You Looking At Me?

The undergrowth was much thicker on this island; the reeds grew tall and strong, reaching high above my head. I had to use my hunting knife as a machete to cut a path through the foliage, and soon I could hear the rustling of animals all around me.

It was really spooky, hearing squeaks and grunts, yaps and hisses, but not being able to see a single creature that made them. Where were they? Could they be dangerous? Was one going to leap out of the undergrowth any minute and grab me? Sweating with fear and effort, I chopped away at the reeds even faster.

But nothing happened – nothing leaped onto my back or came barging through the reeds towards me. Sighing with relief, I soon stepped out of the tall canes into an open area and flopped down onto the grass for a rest.

It was then that I noticed a beady eye staring at me from amongst a clump of bulrushes on the other side of the clearing. It fixed me with an unwavering, unblinking gaze and, fearing another monster attack, I quickly dived behind a gorse bush for cover.

Parting the prickly branches of the gorse, I stared back at the eye, waiting for the creature to make a move. The eye glared blindly out of the bulrushes. It shone like a big ball bearing in the afternoon sun, the small black pupil not moving at all and the eyelid never twitching. *That's strange*, I thought. *It's like the eye of a statue.*

I threw a stone, sending it clattering into the space

between us, but the eye didn't move. I lobbed another stone, this time right into the clump of rushes, but again the eye stayed still. Then, plucking up my courage, I threw another missile, this time straight at the spot where the animal was standing.

Clang! The stone bounced back out of the bulrushes with a metallic ring, and I knew I was right. It *must* be some sort of statue! Creeping out from my hiding place, I walked cautiously into the clearing, waving my arms and stepping from left to right. No, the eye remained motionless – it wasn't looking at me at all; it was just staring into space!

Making a decision, I finally marched straight towards the rushes, ready to scarper at the first sign of trouble. None came, and I pulled the reeds apart and saw the strangest, most welcome sight in the world!

The Sensational Clockwork Swamp Hopper!

It was a tall, slender, silver metal bird, a bit like a stork or a heron, and I knew instantly that it must be one of Jakeman's marvellous mechanical animals – or mechanimals, as he likes to call them.

The bird had a large, pointed and dangerous-looking beak with a nasty barb on the lower bill. A steel horn curved up from its forehead above its blank staring eyes, and its long metal neck was made in hinged sections, enabling it to move and bend. Attached to its jaws was a pair of leather reins for steering. On the mechanimal's back was a big comfy saddle with stirrups for a rider's feet, and a large control panel with an array of buttons and levers. The bird stood on two long thin legs that ended in a pair of splayed feet.

Oh, brilliant! I couldn't wait to try it! If it came from Jakeman, I was sure it was going to help me somehow – although his last invention, the mole, had been a bit of a disappointment! Now, how did this crazy bird work?

I looked it over and saw some paper sticking out from under one of its stubby sheet-metal wings. It was a thin instruction manual, headed:

JAKEMAN'S SENSATIONAL CLOCKWORK SWAMP HOPPER UNRIVALLED AND UNIQUE!

Inside the cover was this tear-out diagram, explaining what all the parts of the bird were for:

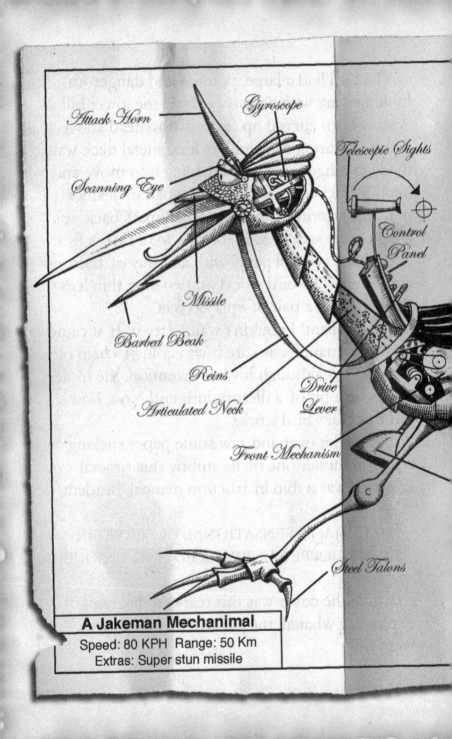

Attack Horn

Gyroscope

Telescopic Sights

Scanning Eye

Control Panel

Missile

Barbed Beak

Reins

Articulated Neck

Drive Lever

Front Mechanism

Steel Talons

A Jakeman Mechanimal

Speed: 80 KPH   Range: 50 Km
Extras: Super stun missile

Jakeman's Sensational
Clockwork Swamp Hopper
Unrivalled & Unique!

Saddle

Main Key

Polished Stainless
Steel Body

Rear Mechanism

Titanium Legs

Large Feet help
spread weight
when walking
on swamp

Stirrups

Patent No: 743681

Testing The Swamp Hopper

As I read the manual, I knew the bird was *just* the thing I needed. According to the booklet, the hopper had been designed to skip across the swamp on its big feet. They acted like snow shoes, distributing the machine's weight across a wide area to enable it to walk across the gluey surface of the bog. Brilliant!

Slipping a foot into one of the stirrups, I swung myself up into the saddle. I took hold of the reins, then pressed a button, pushed a lever forward and waited for the hopper to spring into action. Nothing! *Oh, Jakeman, you blithering banana! Don't say the thing doesn't work!* I looked at the manual again and blushed, because right at the start it said in big, bold lettering:

PLEASE NOTE, THIS MACHINE WON'T WORK UNLESS IT HAS BEEN WOUND UP, YOU BLITHERING BANANA!

Of course, it was a clockwork machine! I checked the diagram and saw that the tail was really a big key. Jumping down, I grabbed it and started to turn. Doh! I'd only turned the key once when the mechanimal sprang forward and went racing across the island, zigzagging like a tall, weedy rugby player: I'd left the lever set to GO! Now I'd have to wait for the mechanism to run down! Luckily I hadn't wound it much and the scatterbrained bird soon slowed and then came to a stop on one slender leg.

I started again, flicking the lever to STOP and winding the tail as much as it would turn. Then, remounting the magnificent machine, I eased the lever forward and the bird immediately took a few stuttering steps. *Whoa!* It wasn't very stable on those matchstick-thin legs; every time it moved, the bird jolted and rocked and I was nearly bumped out of the saddle!

I soon got used to it though, and after practising running up and down the island, I became quite a good hopper jockey. A pull on the reins and the bird moved to the left or right; a forward thrust of the drive lever and the bird accelerated; a sharp yank on the reins and the mechanimal slowed down.

The only problem was that Jakeman had obviously not given the bird a very powerful computer for its brain! Every time a leaf was

What a bird-brain!

zooooom!

blown past it, the hopper
suddenly changed direction and
went scooting off after it. Then, letting
out piercing metallic squawks, it would stab at
the leaf with its vicious beak and nearly throw
me over its head. What a crazy bird!

Soon I was ready though, and,
making sure the tail was fully wound,
I turned the hopper to face the grey-
green swamp and thrust the lever all the
way forward. The mechanimal exploded into
action and went racing towards the water.

Yee-hah! Here we go!

Swamp Hopping

I closed my eyes and held my breath as
the hopper leaped from the shore onto
the water. I fully expected it to sink
like a stone, and for me to end up
floundering about in the monster-
infested swamp. But it didn't!

The bird scooted across the top of the bog, its feet slapping loudly on the weed-clogged surface.

'*Yee-hah!*' I cried. This was more like it, and I steered the bird towards a distant island. Of course, it wasn't that easy, because the empty-headed heron veered this way and that at every minor distraction. We spent half an hour

chasing a feather, and ages when the bird ran round in circles, unsuccessfully trying to catch a purple jumping fish!

Eventually, though, I managed to get the machine more or less under control. We reached the island, raced right across it and off the other end without stopping. I was really motoring now.

The swamp was alive with creatures – animals I'd never seen or heard of before, with weird and wonderful heads, popped out of the slime to look at us as we raced by. Long-necked lugubrious-looking lizards, cantankerous hatchet-clawed crabs and awesome open-jawed alligators snapped and screamed and spat at us as we darted across the bilious bog. I think I even saw a diplodocus . . . but that can't be right, can it?

Every now and then, when we reached an island, I would pull the hopper up and re-wind its motor. Finally, after hours of running flat out,

Was it a diplodocus I saw?

I could see a dark strip of land on the horizon. We were reaching the end of the open swamp. Good! It was not a healthy place and I couldn't wait to be back on dry land.

The sun was sinking low in the sky – it would soon be time to find another place to sleep. The islands became more and more numerous, while the channels between them grew narrower and narrower; soon the swamp turned to sticky mud and we were on solid ground again.

A Garden Of Beautiful Flowers — Not!

Mangrove trees filled the muddy landscape, and now there were the most amazing plants growing all around them: little white flowers covered the ground, twinkling like diamonds in the setting sun; ferns with leaves as big as umbrellas clustered under the base of the trees; and giant plants stood taller than me, their huge drooping heads of brilliant petals hanging from dark green stems.

The scent was intoxicating, and everything looked so peaceful I decided it would be the perfect place to spend the night. The giant flowers curved overhead, creating natural shelters, so I made my bed beneath them. That was a big mistake . . .

Ouch! What was that? No sooner had I lain down than I felt something grab me violently by the ankle. Yikes! One of the plant's thick hairy tendrils had snaked across the ground and was wrapping itself around my leg. I tried to kick it off but it was too strong. Help! As it started to pull me across the ground, the plant bowed its head and the rubbery petals opened. Inside I could see rotting bones floating in a pool of foaming juices. Oh no, I had camped in a bed of flesh-eating flowers!

Eek! I'm being eaten by a ferocious flower!

I had to act quickly. I needed my knife and made a desperate grab for my rucksack, but it was already out of reach. What on earth was I going to do? Then, as my feet disappeared into the flower head, my hand knocked against a stone. I picked it up and hurled it at the swamp hopper. *Clang!* What a shot – it knocked the drive lever forward and the bird sprang into action.

CLUNK!

What a shot!

It went scooting through the trees, running in circles and honking its mechanical call until, attracted by the rocking plant, it made a beeline towards us. Then, *chip-chop*, the hopper started pecking at the plant's thick stem in a mad frenzy. It recoiled and writhed and I was lifted clean off the ground as the tendril flapped me about in the air like a flag in a hurricane! Again and again the hopper chopped at the stem until, finally, it broke and the flower came crashing down.

'Phew, that was close!' I cried. In a mad panic, I grabbed my stuff and leaped onto the back of the hopper. Then, with a sharp yank on the reins, I steered my mechanical saviour away through the trees.

It was getting dark now but, remembering something I'd read in the instruction manual, I flicked a switch and the bird's eyes sent out two powerful beams of light. Brilliant! Now we could really get some speed up, and I didn't stop the hopper until we'd left the deadly carnivorous plants far, far behind.

Soon the ground underneath grew drier; tall, broadleaved oaks replaced the mangrove trees and I found myself deep in a quiet forest. By the light from the hopper's eyes I've just finished jotting down my latest escapade, and now I'm going to climb onto a high branch and get some kip.

Phoning Home (can you hear me, mum?)

I woke up bright and early the next morning and was soon nipping through the forest on my metal pal. It was a lovely day, with birds twittering all around; it was almost like being back home, going for a walk in the woods with Mum and Dad, and this prompted me to try and phone Mum again.

Every time I ring, it's always the day I first set out on my exploring adventures – even though I've been away for four hundred years! And Mum always says the same old thing: *Don't be late for tea and remember to pick up a pint of milk on the way home!*

The last time I rang her, though, she started going on about me having missed tea and said that there was a strange man in a long black coat knocking on the door! I started to panic – it sounded just like my arch enemy Joseph Craik – and told her *not* to answer the door. But Mum had already hung up.

I dialled the number.

'Oh, hello, darling, is everything all right?' Mum asked.

'Well, apart from being attacked by a slime monster and nearly eaten by a carnivorous carnation, everything's fine,' I said. 'But, Mum, who was that at the door—?'

'Sounds wonderful, dear,' continued Mum,

Sounds wonderful dear...

not answering my question. 'Oh, wait a minute, Charlie. Here's your dad just come in. Now remember, don't be late for tea—'

'Mum, can you hear me?' I called, but the line had gone dead. Darn it! Oh well, things *seemed* to be back to normal; at least Joseph Craik hadn't answered the phone at my house and I could stop worrying so much.

I pushed the hopper's lever forward and we whizzed along through the thick forest. Warm sunlight filtered down through the foliage overhead, and the machine's feet padded silently over a deep bed of moss, throwing up clouds of leafy dust.

Forest Trufflers

We travelled for hours, and the forest went on and on. I started to notice that the earth was scarred and pitted; shallow trenches crisscrossed the forest floor as if a mini bulldozer had been let loose there. *That's weird*, I thought. *What would churn up the ground like that?*

The ground was scarred with shallow trenches

As we came to a clearing, I heard grunting noises and saw a flash of movement beyond the fringe of trees. I reined in the swamp hopper and dismounted, peering into the clearing from behind a bush.

I could see a group of orange, bristly backs poking up above a tall patch of spiky grass. The creatures grunted and snuffled and barked. As they moved out onto a patch of dried mud, I saw what they were: forest pigs! Large porkers with great sagging bellies. They looked big and powerful, with long snouts and great yellow tusks that curved up and over their noses.

They forced their muzzles into the earth and shuffled forward, carving long furrows in the ground, until they turned up a tasty root or a succulent forest truffle. Then, with much squealing and snorting, they devoured the prize and continued their noisy search. They looked a bit like the trufflegrumpers (useless, smelly things!) I'd seen in Gorilla City, and I decided to name these porcine creatures trufflers!

Just then I felt something nudge my leg and, looking down, saw a little baby truffler staring up at

A little baby truffler stared up at me

me with quizzical eyes. It pushed its damp nose against my hand and grunted. *Oh, how cute*, I thought, and rubbed the little chap's stripy back. The truffler closed its eyes in satisfaction and nuzzled closer to me.

'Hello, little fella,' I cooed, chucking it under the chin. 'What do you want – a cuddle?'

I picked the baby truffler up, but as soon as it was in my arms, the contrary critter let out the most high-pitched squeal I've ever heard. It

Mummy truffler

sounded like a kettle singing fit to burst!

'Shh!' I whispered. 'There's no need for that.' I was just about to put the complaining toddler back on the ground when *CRASH!* mummy truffler came barging through the undergrowth. When it saw its mum, the baby truffler let out an even louder and more pitiful squeal, and she charged straight towards me, grunting ferociously. *Yikes!*

I rolled out of the way as she bore down on me, her snout pulled back in a snarl and her tusks glinting. I got to my feet and ran towards the hopper, leaping into the saddle and thrusting the drive lever forward to GO! Mummy truffler flew on past, then turned and came racing back, cutting off my retreat through the trees. Panicking, I steered the bird into the clearing and realized straight away that I'd made a big blunder, because big daddy truffler was standing there, pawing the ground like an angry bull!

Trufflers Gone Wild! Help!

With a ferocious bellow the great boar charged and the whole pack followed. There were furious trufflers coming at me from all directions.

I drove the hopper forward, weaving a path through the angry mob. My scatterbrained friend was knocked and barged and buffeted, and it was hard to hold on as we were rocked to and fro by the marauding pigs. I tried to make a run for cover, but a small group of snorters herded us back to the centre of the clearing again.

Then the big daddy hit us a glancing blow and one of the swamp hopper's legs buckled. *Oh no!* It was impossible to steer the thing with a bent leg. I pulled the bird up and turned to face my foe. The pigs had lined up about twenty metres away, preparing for a mass charge. With a loud snort from the boar, the whole platoon powered forward, grunting and squealing, hooves pounding. Now was the time to use the swamp hopper's secret weapon!

As big daddy led the marauding horde towards me, I leaned forward and got him in

the telescopic sights attached to the saddle.
This was one of the most extraordinary things
I had discovered in the operating instructions:

Big daddy
truffler

the swamp hopper could fire little stun missiles from its nostrils. They didn't do any permanent damage, but were capable of stunning anything from an ox to a bear!

I waited till the truffler's big bony head was in the cross-hairs of the sights, and *boof!* I pushed the FIRE button. A red streak shot from the hopper's nostril, and *BAM!* It hit big bad daddy right on the forehead.

'*Wheee!*' he squealed. The rest of the pigs skidded to a halt, but big daddy carried on; I saw his legs wobble and his eyes cross, but he didn't stop!

Only when he was almost upon us did his legs finally fold, and he went crashing to the ground. His speed carried him on, though, and the massive bulk of the comatose pig hit us at full pelt. The swamp hopper went flying in one direction; I went flying in the other, hitting the ground and tumbling over and over. I came to a halt near the edge of the clearing, and looked around for my metal friend. Oh blow! There was no hope for the poor thing. It was lying in a heap of broken parts and the trufflers were pulling the metal sheeting apart and trampling it under their trotters.

Big daddy started to come out of his daze; seeing me, he heaved himself up and charged again. *Oh, flippin' heck – doesn't he ever give up?* I didn't hang about, but jumped up, grabbed an overhanging bough and swung myself up into a tree. I scuttled along to the trunk and climbed higher into the broad oak. Then, with a leap and a Tarzan yodel, I dived onto an outstretched branch and began swinging through the forest like my good pals the gorillas had taught me so long ago!

Big daddy truffler followed me, snorting and barging against the wide tree trunks with his bullet head, trying to knock me out of the branches.

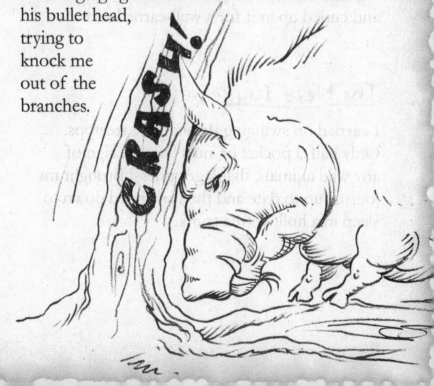

But after a while he gave up, thank goodness, and I continued my journey alone. I'd lost a good ally in the swamp hopper; it might have been a bit daft, but it had helped me escape from the swamp – *and* saved me from the man-eating flowers. Although I know it was only a rather annoying machine, I am going to miss the company!

All afternoon, I swung through the forest canopy. Every now and then I would surprise a squirrel, or a fat pigeon, and send them scuttling away through the branches. At nightfall I found a big abandoned crow's nest and curled up in it for a well-earned rest.

The Next Day

I carried on swinging through the treetops. Only half a pocket of nuts left. No sign of any wild animals, thank goodness! Brought my journal up to date and then snuggled down to sleep in a hollow tree trunk.

Tweet tweet I'm a little birdy
I'm going daft in this never ending forest!
I'm swinging through the trees, just swinging through the trees
Charlie Small woz 'ere
Gunge
This forest seems to go on forever!
Jakeman where are yooooo?
Big cissy
I hate Ma-mite
Old Slimy

Who Goes There?

I set off first thing in the morning and carried on swinging through the forest. By early evening my arms were getting tired and I was very thirsty. My water bottle was just about empty, so when I heard the welcome sound of running water, I climbed down until I was standing amongst the lower branches of a big ash.

I didn't want to surprise another herd of trufflers, so I sat on a wide bough and studied the forest floor below. It looked deserted; there was a patch of leaf-strewn grass, rising to form a low bank and – oh, good – beyond the bank was a tinkling stream.

After taking another recce for danger, I jumped down and crept cautiously across the sward to the stream. I sat down amongst a group of trees on the bank, cupping my hands in the brook and taking a long swig. Oh, it was wonderful! The water was cool and crystal clear, and I took gulp after gulp; I splashed my face, washing away the slime and grime and spittle I'd collected since flying out of the Underworld; finally, not being able to resist it, I took off my holey trainers and lay down in the gushing chill, letting the water wash over me, cleaning my clothes and myself at the same time!

Feeling refreshed, and cleaner than I've ever been since leaving home, I climbed up onto the bank and lay down to let myself dry in the warm afternoon breeze. Soon I drifted off into a light snooze. I dreamed of slime monsters, troglodytes, desperados and home—

A cracking of twigs woke me with a start!

'Who's there?' I asked dozily, but I couldn't see anything beyond the trees that clustered around me. *That's funny*, I thought. *Surely these trees weren't growing so close to me before I went to sleep. Well, of course they were! Trees don't move about of their own accord, do they?* I heard another rustle of leaves and the definite snap of twigs.

'Hey,' I said, 'who goes there?' I was starting to get nervous. I'm sure the trees were much closer to me than before. I got warily to my feet and started to edge away, crouching in the undergrowth and looking around for signs of approaching danger.

I waited and watched, but nothing happened.

What sort of creature is hiding in the undergrowth?

No rogue animal came padding through the trees; no man-eating plant sent out a coiling runner to wind itself around my ankle and drag me into its greedy petal mouth. I waited some more and then some more, but still nothing happened and I started to relax.

Then the undergrowth rustled and shook, and all of a sudden a little grey streak shot out from the ferns. I nearly jumped out of my skin and my heart started to beat hard as the animal stopped just where I'd been sleeping. I breathed a sigh of relief. It was a rabbit! A little bundle of soft grey fur, and it started nibbling nervously at the grass, its pointy ears twitching.

I chuckled to myself. Imagine being frightened of a rabbit; what a fearless explorer I was! It's strange how your mind plays tricks on you, I thought, because now I was sure the trees hadn't moved an inch; it was just my imagination. I shifted my weight and the noise startled the anxious bunny; it shot off into the undergrowth again.

Feeling rather foolish, I grabbed my rucksack, ready to set off. I had no idea which way to go, so I got out the compass I had found on the skeleton in the gorillas' jungle. According to Jakeman's map, his factory was in the north-west, but that would only be of use if I knew exactly where I was now, and that's very difficult to judge with a largely blank map!

How could I pinpoint my position? Surely it was something to do with the stars, but I would need a sextant to work it out and I didn't have one of those in my kit! I would just have to carry on going north-west and hope I ended up *somewhere* near the factory. Sooner or later I was bound to meet someone I could ask.

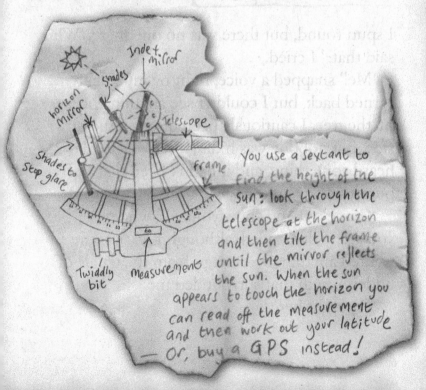

Index mirror

shades

horizon mirror

Telescope

frame

Shades to stop glare

Twiddly bit

measurements

You use a sextant to find the height of the sun: look through the telescope at the horizon and then tilt the frame until the mirror reflects the sun. When the sun appears to touch the horizon you can read off the measurement and then work out your latitude — Or, buy a GPS instead!

As I packed up my rucksack, I noticed my multi-tooled penknife and thought, *I know, I'll leave my mark – then if anyone is out looking for me, whether it's Jakeman or someone from home, they will know I've been this way.* I opened the blade and went to carve my name in the trunk of one of the trees.

'Don't even think about it, buster,' said a dry, crackly voice.

The Tree People!

I spun round, but there was no one there. 'Who said that?' I cried.

'Me!' snapped a voice, right by my side. I turned back, but I couldn't see anything because of the tree. I cautiously peered round the other side, but nobody was hiding there. I *knew* I'd heard something, and it hadn't been that fluffy bunny!

'Come out and show yourself, whoever you are,' I demanded, although I wasn't sure I wanted anything to emerge from the tangle of undergrowth that surrounded me.

'I'm right here.'

'Where?' I cried, starting to think I was going mad.

'Here,' said a voice coming from the tree, and as I looked up into the branches to see if anyone was sitting there, I saw two eyes staring out of the tree's bark!

'A talking tree!' I gulped in amazement. 'You've got to be joking. A talking tree with eyes!'

With that the tree took a pace forward, moving its branches and shaking its leaves. Then another tree moved, and another, and soon the whole grove I had slept amongst was swaying and moving with a crackle of twigs.

I stepped back, looking for an escape route, but as I did so a twiggy hand came to rest on my shoulder.

'Don't worry,' rasped the tree. 'Won't harm you. Peaceful beings.'

'But you're trees,' I said again, feeling confused and more than a little crazy.

'No, not trees. Human – human plants!'

Then, as I looked more closely, I began to see what he meant. Yes, they looked like trees: their skin was gnarled and creased like bark; but they only had two branches and these were really their arms, which ended in big twiggy-fingered hands. They had faces and mouths and— *Oh wow!* This was really creepy!

'Don't be alarmed,' croaked the tree in short, snapping sentences. 'Forest dwellers. Lived in woods for centuries. Started out just like you. Evolved into different species: tree men.'

It was strange, but the more I looked at these weird creatures, the more they looked like people! Some were tall – maybe as much as four metres high; others were wide and squat, hardly any taller than a regular person. Their fingers were like branches, covered with little offshoots of twigs, and their hair was a tangled mass of shoots, thick with leaves. Even their noses ended in gnarly knots and twiggy protuberances, and their trunks were clothed in drapes of lichens and moss. Here's a sketch I did of one of the tree people:

_____

'How many of you are there?' I asked.

'Few tribes in whole forest. Ten of us in tribe.'

'Yes, I can make you all out quite clearly now,' I said. 'Do you have names?'

'Of course! Or things' – and he paused to take a long rasping breath – 'confusing. My name Tree!'

'Oh, that must make things much clearer,' I said.

A Promise Of Help

'You are lost?' asked Tree. 'Can we help?'

'Oh, yes please,' I cried, and told him of my journey to Jakeman's factory. I showed him the map, but it didn't mean much to him or his friends.

'Don't know Jakeman,' crackled Tree, and I sighed in disappointment. 'But know man to help.'

'You do?' I cried. 'Does he live in this forest? Does he know Jakeman personally?'

'Calm down,' chuckled Tree, with a sound like snapping twigs. 'Man lives far away. In Frozen North. Very clever; knows where everyone lives. Name is Mamuk.'

'But if he's in the Frozen North, how on earth am I going to find him?' I said, growing frustrated. 'It'll take me ages to get there; if I don't get lost on the way, that is!'

'Don't worry,' rasped the tree man. 'Have friend; ask nicely, she take you there.'

'D'you think so? Oh, brilliant!' I cried, and a flock of startled birds clattered up through the forest.

'Need anything else?'

'I'm rather hungry,' I said. 'I don't suppose you have something to eat?'

'Follow me.'

'You can walk as well!' I exclaimed as the tree people moved closer to the stream.

'Of course,' said the tree man, raising a gnarled foot. 'How else move about?'

'I'm sorry – I keep forgetting that you're people, not trees!'

'Here,' said Tree as he stepped into a muddy puddle and closed his eyes in pleasure. 'Lovely,' he said.

'I've already had a wash. I'm more hungry than dirty.'

'This food,' said Tree. 'Full of nutrients. Mmm, delicious! Suck up through feet!'

With that the tree man lifted his leg again. I could see a network of fine roots growing from the sole of his foot.

Incredible! These things really had evolved into true forest dwellers. They were as much trees as they were people.

'I'm afraid I haven't got roots,' I said. 'Only a mouth, and I had more than enough mud in the Underworld. You wouldn't happen to have any fruit to eat, would you?'

'No!' said Tree, and all his friends rustled their leaves indignantly. 'Not cannibals! But have mushrooms.'

'Oh, I'm not sure about that,' I said. 'Some of them are deadly poisonous, and I wouldn't know which were OK to eat.'

'Don't fret. We know,' said Tree. 'Ashley, pick mushrooms for friend . . . name?'

'I'm Charlie Small,' I said. 'Thank you, Ashley,' I called as a very small tree person wandered off through the forest, grumbling to himself.

'Why me?' he rustled. '*Ashley, do this. Ashley, fetch that.*'

'Don't worry,' said Tree with a dry, rustling laugh. 'He prickly!'

Lovely Grub *mmm!*

Ashley soon returned with a great big pile of mushrooms. Now, I'm not usually that keen on them, but I was *very* hungry, so I bit into a small nut-brown mushroom, expecting it to taste yuk! But it didn't – it tasted of delicious creamy marshmallow! Mmm!

I tried a different one, and this tasted of roast beef and gravy; another was just like burger and chips, and soon I had scoffed my way through the whole pile.

'Thank you, Ashley,' I said, nursing a very full tummy. 'Thank you, Tree.'

'OK, Charlie,' said Tree. 'Now sleep. Long night ahead. Friend come at midnight.'

Yum yum!

Fantastic! I couldn't wait; I do hope Tree's friend agrees to take me to Mamuk. I knew Tree was right: I *should* get some rest. So now I'm just finishing writing my journal and snuggling down in a heap of old leaves. My new friends the tree people will guard me while I sleep and wake me when my guide arrives – whoever she is!

Octavia Moon

A spiky hand shook me by the shoulder and I
dozily opened my eyes. Tree was standing over me.

'Wake up, Charlie. Time to go,' he said.

I yawned and rubbed my eyes. 'Is it midnight
already?' I asked sleepily.

'Past midnight. Octavia waiting. Must hurry.'

'Brilliant!' I said, wondering if my guide was one
of the tree people, or a human like me. I looked
around for her, but I couldn't see anybody at all.
'Where is she?' I asked.

'In chestnut tree,' croaked Tree.

'That's a funny place to wait!' I said.

'Not for owl,' Tree replied.

'An owl? How's an owl going to help me?'

'Octavia Moon tundra owl,' said Tree.
'Powerful, clever, brave. Don't keep her waiting.
Very grumpy!' Then, with a rasping cackle, he
added, 'But her hoot . . . worse than her bite!'

Tree held out a twiggy hand and I put my foot
onto it; with a heave-ho, he hoisted me up over
his head until he was at full stretch and I was
balancing on his palm, a good four metres from
the ground.

'Meet Octavia Moon,' he said, placing me on one of the chestnut's branches.

Octavia Moon was as big as me

Yikes! I was so glad Tree had said Octavia was friendly, because if I'd just happened to bump into her, I would have run a million miles! She was that scary looking!

I stepped onto the branch and found myself staring into two bright yellow eyes as big as saucers and level with mine. *Crikey, she's as tall as me!* I thought. Two long and feathery eyebrows sprouted from above the owl's headlamp eyes, giving her a stern and intimidating expression, and in the middle of her wide face curved a cruel-looking beak. Out of the side of her beak hung a long wriggling tail.

'Woo-who are you?' asked the bird. 'Don't you know it's roo-hude to interrupt a lady while she's eating?'

Oh, really! I thought. Surely the tree folk had told her all about me. She was just being awkward. Then I realized she had asked me a question!

'You can talk!' I said in amazement.

'And why shouldn't I be able to-hoo talk? Owls are very intelligent birds you-hoo know.'

'Oh, of course, sorry! I'm Charlie: Charlie Small. I'm pleased to meet you, Octavia,' I said very politely, for she had the sort of appearance that instinctively made you well-behaved.

The owl blinked and gulped at the same time, and the mouse-tail disappeared like a string of spaghetti. 'Madam Moon to-hoo you,' she said, and then started to choke and cough and retch, all at the same time.

'Are you OK?' I asked, edging along the branch to pat her between her feathery shoulders.

'*Oooheeaggherrr!*' she choked, bringing up a furry ball and spitting it out. Charming!

bits of bone from rodents and birds

hair, fur and feathers

Owls bring up pellets of undigested fur and bone - Yuk!

'Beg pardon: pellet,' she said, by way of explanation. 'You must be the boy who wants to-hoo go to the Frozen North. Then hurry up and climb on my back, Charlie. There's no time to-hoo lose!'

I squeezed behind the plump Madam Moon and jumped up, clinging around her fat neck, piggyback style.

'Is that OK?' I started to say, but Octavia Moon had already taken off, swooping out of the tree and climbing up into the night sky. *Yahoo!* I grabbed a handful of feathers and held on tight.

'Cheerio, and thank you!' I called down to the tree folk, and I heard their dry, crackly replies.

''Bye, Charlie. Good luck.'

Night Flight

We climbed higher and higher, up towards the wispy clouds that scudded across a deep indigo sky. Below me the forest stretched out in all directions, lit by the pale light from a big lemony moon.

'You-hoo must hold on tight, Charlie,' hooted

Octavia. 'It's a long way down!'

We travelled for miles; gradually the forest started to thin below us, and then, suddenly, it was gone. In its place lay a soft, hilly terrain. I could make out a wide ribbon of river that sparkled like silver as it wound its way between the grassy hummocks.

On we flew. Again the scenery changed as the hills gave way to a flat, barren plain, with fantastic-shaped rock formations rising from the ground like weird sculptures. In the deep shadows cast by the moon it was easy to imagine these outcrops as huge slumbering giants, great severed fists, or fearsome fossilized dragons.

'*Yikes!*' I yelled as Octavia Moon suddenly dropped away beneath me in a steep dive. 'What are you doing? *Arrgh!*' The wind whistled in my ears as we hurtled towards the rock-strewn ground. 'I'm slipping. Madam Moon, I'm slipping!'

The owl didn't reply, and I grabbed the feathers on the nape of her neck even tighter and lay flat against her back to avoid being

blown off. As I clung on for dear life, she
hunched her shoulders and fell almost vertically
out of the sky.

The ground rushed up towards us and I thought we were going to be dashed against the rocks. Then, at the very last second, Octavia levelled out and I heard a small squeak as she extended her powerful clawed feet. We swooped up again, landing on the top of a rocky crag, and I lay panting in fear and exhilaration as the owl lifted a small rodent to her beak.

'Snack time,' said Octavia Moon casually. 'Do-hoo you want some?'

'No thanks,' I stuttered, still shaking. 'I've still got some mushrooms.' But I felt too queasy to eat anything.

Snowstorm

As we continued on our journey, I got Jakeman's map out and, balancing precariously on Octavia's shoulders, started to fill in some of the unexplored region. I'm not sure if I've put the details in the right places and my drawing is very wobbly, but it gives some sort of idea where I've been, and will be good to have as a reference when I get back home and want to remember all my travels. This is it so far:

The frozen North?
UNKNOWN REGION
PROBABLY VERY DANGEROUS
Yikes!
Fantastic shaped rocks
Tree people about here?
BEWARE
Forest
Forest
High Plateau
Slime monster
help!
my rocket powered flight
Mountains
Desert
Woosh!
Tubes into the Underworld
N
BEWARE!

The air had turned very chilly and I pulled the owl's feathery ruff of feathers over my knees like a blanket.

'How much further?' I called.

'An hour or two-hoo,' came the owl's reply.

'What do you think the temperature is?' I asked as my teeth started to chatter.

'About two-hoo degrees,' said Octavia. 'But it's going to get chilly soo-hoon.'

'Soon?' I cried. 'It's freezing already!'

'Don't boo-hoo like a baby,' huffed Octavia. 'What will you-hoo be like when we get to the Frozen North?'

Blimey, Tree was right. She was a bit grumpy! I pulled my coat and the holey scarf out of my explorer's kit and put them on. My face was starting to go numb, and ice was starting to form in my eyebrows and on the end of my nose. Then snowflakes started to fall, thick and fast.

In a second the sky turned white as the driving snow made crazy patterns in front of my eyes, making me feel dizzy and disorientated. Octavia flew on, but a strong wind started to blow; we were buffeted about and it was difficult to keep on course.

'Twit-twoo! We're in . . .' shrieked my guide, but her words were blown away by the wind. Then, *whoosh!* The snowstorm hit us with all its might, flinging us up through the swirling sky. Octavia tumbled, then righted herself, and then was blown tail over tip, tumbling back down.

Whoosh! The storm raged; the snow churned, and we were thrown about like clothes in a tumble drier.

'Woo! Watch out, Charlie!' cried Octavia, and on juddering wings she spiralled out of the sky.

Oof! We crash-landed with a thump and I dropped into a deep drift of snow. Immediately the wind lifted me clean off the ground, and I grabbed hold of a narrow rock to avoid being blown away.

'We'll have to wait here until the storm has passed,' I yelled at Octavia. She was desperately trying to stay upright in the howling wind, head down and wings tucked in.

'You-hoo are on your own from here,' she called back. 'You-hoo must go that way.' She lifted a wing to point, and immediately a gust of wind caught her and blew her away into the stormy dawn. 'Woooooh!'

'*Come back!*' I yelled. 'Don't leave me here

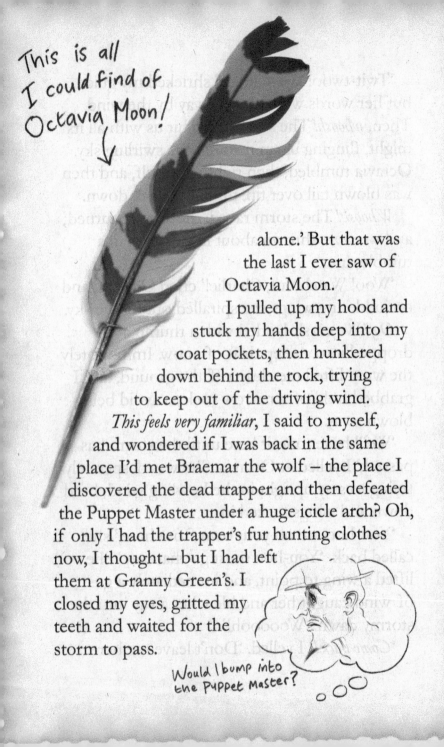

This is all I could find of Octavia Moon! ↓

alone.' But that was the last I ever saw of Octavia Moon.

I pulled up my hood and stuck my hands deep into my coat pockets, then hunkered down behind the rock, trying to keep out of the driving wind.

This feels very familiar, I said to myself, and wondered if I was back in the same place I'd met Braemar the wolf – the place I discovered the dead trapper and then defeated the Puppet Master under a huge icicle arch? Oh, if only I had the trapper's fur hunting clothes now, I thought – but I had left them at Granny Green's. I closed my eyes, gritted my teeth and waited for the storm to pass.

Would I bump into the Puppet Master?

A Stranger In The Snow

As a pink sun rose in the sky, the wind dropped, the snow eased and I could come out from behind my rock and take a look around. The whole area was covered in a deep blanket of snow, smoothing out the fantastic rock formations and making them look as if they had been carved from marble.

I was standing above a huge drop, looking down upon a wide, flat-bottomed canyon, with soaring cliffs on both sides and snow-covered woods dotting the valley floor. I couldn't see any sign of a village or even a house but, as it looked more sheltered down in the valley, I decided that's the way I would go.

It was an easy climb down the rocky side, and I soon reached the bottom. Taking out a hot-cross-bun-flavoured mushroom to chew on, I set off through the snow, not really knowing where I was going but hoping to meet someone who could tell me where I would find this Mamuk character.

I trudged for miles along the valley floor, keeping a sharp lookout for my old friend

Braemar, but not really expecting to see him. Although I was in an icy, snow-laden country, the landscape looked quite different from the chilly wasteland where I'd met the brave white wolf.

The snow continued to fall, but less thickly now, and as my path climbed up towards two large outcrops of rock, a figure stepped out and stood silhouetted against the pale sky. *Oh, good,* I thought. *Here's someone who may be able to give me directions.* As I hurried towards him, I noticed he had a red silk scarf covering his face. *That's odd,* I thought. *It's not that cold any more.*

'Mmm, mmm, mm, mmm!' said the masked man.

'I beg your pardon?' I said. 'Your voice is a bit muffled behind that hanky.'

The figure pulled a pistol from his belt and levelled it at me. 'I said, stand and deliver, you nincompoop. Your money or your life!'

Yikes! A highwayman – this could be tricky! Play it cool, Charlie, try to keep calm. Still, he couldn't take what I hadn't got, could he?

'I don't have any money,' I said, patting my pockets. 'I'm stony broke!'

'Oh dear, let's do it the hard way then.

Yikes! It was a horrible highwayman

Turn out your pockets,' drawled the stranger, sounding bored. Despite his appearance, he had a rather posh voice. He was dressed in clothes that, although once very fine, were now somewhat threadbare and worn. He wore an incredible cone-shaped hat, a dark green jacket, and heavy brown trousers tucked into a pair of soft leather boots. I couldn't see much of his face as it was hidden behind the red silk scarf.

I pulled my pockets inside out. Apart from a few swamp nuts, he could see they were empty and he tutted and scratched his head.

'Typical!' he said. 'The only person I've met on the road all morning and he hasn't got a bloomin' bean to his name. This puts me in a

Hand it over

tricky situation, lad. Boss Belcher, leader of the barbarous brigands, is expecting me to return with a decent haul of loot. What am I going to say to him? I can't be the only brigand to return empty-handed again! My pals are bound to get something and I'll end up looking a right twit!'

'Well, I'm really sorry I haven't got anything for you to steal,' I said sarcastically.

'Oh, never mind. I'll just have to take that bag. At least it's something. Come on, hand it over.'

'Not my rucksack!' I cried, panicking. 'I need it. It's got all my explorer's stuff inside.'

'I can't help that, lad. I need it as well. Now come on, hand it over.' The brigand pointed his gun right at me. 'I'm losing my patience,' he said.

Angrily I shrugged the rucksack off my back and threw it over to him. 'Satisfied?' I asked.

The brigand picked it up and tucked it under his arm. 'There's no need to get so annoyed. I'm only doing my job!' said the rascally robber politely. 'You really shouldn't be out alone, anyway. It's not safe around here, y'know!'

'Is that so?' I sneered.

'It is indeed,' said the robber, chuckling. 'Toodle-oo!'

With that he disappeared behind the rocks; a few seconds later I heard the muffled sound of a horse's hooves cantering away.

'Darn it! Dash it and double drat!' I yelled, kicking the snow. What was I going to do without my explorer's kit? It had saved my skin time and time again and I felt very vulnerable without it.

Luckily I'd stuffed my pencil and this journal in my coat pocket when I was still with the tree people, so I flopped down in the snow to write up my latest adventures and have a good think about what to do next . . .

Right, that's enough thinking! I've decided that there's only one thing I can do: I must track down the brazen brigand and *steal my rucksack back*! I'll write more later.

More Brigands And Another Robbery Oh no!

It wasn't difficult to track the barbarous brigand. His horse had left clear hoof prints in the snow and I followed them across the undulating valley floor for some hours.

After a while, things became a bit trickier.

? horse Hoof prints

Other hoof prints appeared and the tracks of my prey got lost amongst them. Some were made by horses, but most were quite different: they were cloven, like a cow's hooves. The droppings in the area made me think they weren't cattle prints, though. These were small, three-centimetre-long pellets, whereas we all know a cow does a great big dollop!

I was zigzagging across the snow, trying to pick up the trail, when I heard a horse whinny a little distance away. I crouched down low and crept towards a large snow-covered mound, where I thought the noise came from. Yes – now I could hear voices, and I crept quietly up the side of the mound and peered over the top.

There, sitting on his horse below me, was the brigand who had taken my rucksack. I could see it hooked over the pommel of his fancy saddle. He wasn't alone, though; there were two other brigands, also on horseback, both with scarves over their mouths to conceal their identity. They had pistols trained on a fourth man who was dressed in a baggy hooded suit of tan-coloured animal hides.

He sat on a rickety-looking sledge made of wooden poles lashed together with leather ties. Stacked behind him were piles of animal skins, and harnessed to the front of the sleigh was a team of half a dozen shaggy-coated reindeer. So that's what had made the hoof prints! I thought. They had magnificent antlers and were breathing hard as if they had recently been galloping.

As the brigands dismounted from their horses and started to search through the skins on the sleigh, the man turned his head and I could see his face poking out from his fur-edged hood. He had a long fringe of white hair above his narrow, almond-shaped eyes, and a pale, wispy, pointed beard jutting from his chin.

He looks like a Nenet tribesman – a reindeer herder, I thought. I'd read about them in one of

The reindeer herder

my explorer books at home. They graze their massive herds of reindeer all over the tundra, using their hides for clothes, their meat for food and their antlers to make tools.

'Let me go, you numbskulls. I'm in a hurry,' the deer herder was saying. 'Frozen fishtails! How many times do I have to say, I don't have anything to give you?'

Ay Carumba!

'Ay carumba! We
don't belieeeve you,
Meester
Reindeer Man,'
said one of
the brigands,
who was short
and plump and
spoke with a strong
accent. 'We know who
you are. We recognize you
straight away. You're ze leader of *all*
ze reindeer herders – ze big, big cheese! Don't
try and tell us you don't have ze cash stashed
away somewhere. We're taking you to ze boss.
He'll make you talk, Meester Mamuk.'

'Mamuk!' I gasped. This was the man the
tree people said might help me, and now these
barbarous brigands were taking him away.

'We'll keep zese skins, though – and ze
reindeer as well. Highway robbery is hungry
work and they'll make us ze fine feast!'

One of the brigands led the deer by the
reins, while the other two trotted along beside
the sledge, their guns trained on the hapless
herder. I followed behind, darting from rock to

tree for cover, and following their deep tracks
in the snow. I couldn't afford to lose them now.
Mamuk may be the only person who can help
me find Jakeman. First, though, it seems as
if I am going to have to help him escape the
clutches of these barbarous brigands!

The Brigands' Lair At Frostbite Pass

I tracked the brigands as they led the herder
across the valley floor to the opposite side,
where they disappeared into a small evergreen
forest. Here the ground rose in a series of
towering cliffs. The air was thick with the
perfume of pine trees and made me feel quite
dizzy.

They had no idea I was following them and
made no attempt to keep quiet. I could hear the
brigands laughing and joking, the crack of twigs
under their horses' hooves, and the creaking and
thumping of the sleigh as the reindeer hauled it
over the web of tree roots on the forest floor.

I followed them along a rough track through
the trees until it led us up a steep slope and
into a great V-shaped fault in the moss-covered

cliff-face. As I entered the crevice, I saw a small weathered sign hammered into a rock. Rubbing away the moss and dirt that covered it, I saw the inscription:

Underneath the lettering, someone had scratched a skull and crossbones into the wood. *Mmm*, I thought, *that's not very welcoming*, but I had no choice but to carry on.

Although the path was quite narrow here – the sleigh must have only just been able to squeeze through – there was snow underfoot again and the brigands could urge the reindeer on. Soon I was left a long way behind. I didn't mind, though; their tracks were still easy to make out in the fresh fall of snow.

I'd been stumbling along for about an hour when the winding track turned a corner and the pass widened out. A huge lonesome pine stood in the middle, and I crept behind its wide trunk and surveyed the scene. The ground sloped away from me – a wide expanse of pristine snow bordered by soaring craggy sides. The tracks of the brigands' horses and the herder's sleigh snaked away down the slope towards a pile of massive boulders on my left, and poking above them I could just make out a small metal chimney sending up a thin plume of smoke. I had reached the brigands' lair!

I crawled along the ground, making sure the boulders shielded me from the brigands' hideout. Silently scaling the slippery rocks and creeping over the boulders on my tummy, I found myself looking down on a large, rickety wooden hut. A porch ran along the front of the building, and on a chair by the door sat the brigand who had stolen my rucksack, scanning the empty pass for intruders. Luckily he hadn't been doing a very good job!

Directly below me, joined to the side of the brigands' cabin, was a fenced-off corral where the herder's reindeer were penned, nervously pacing up and down. Above this, high in the apex of the cabin's wall, was a single window that stood slightly ajar. If I could climb up to

A snow leopard
watched my every move →

Reindeer
poo!

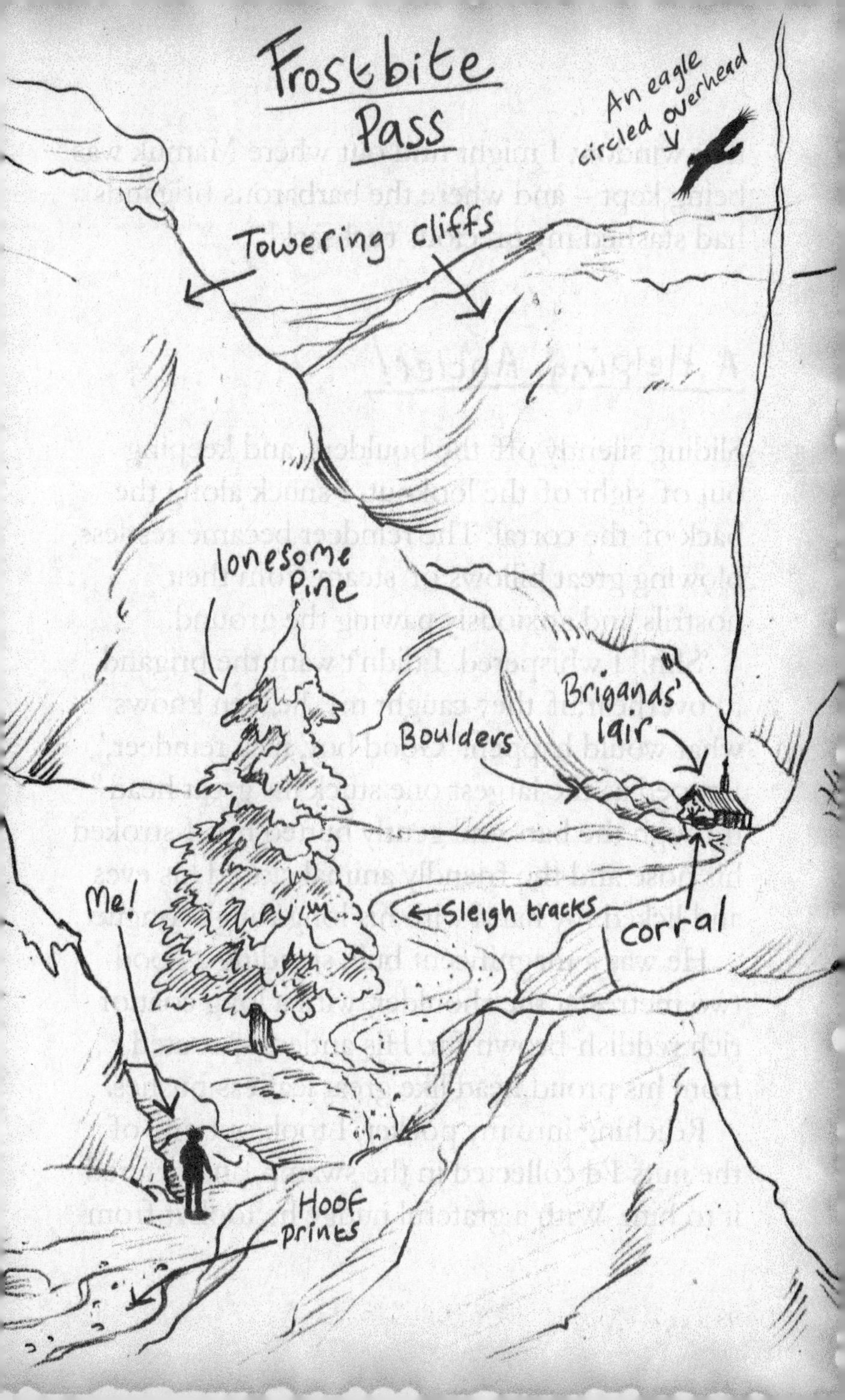

Frostbite Pass

An eagle circled overhead ↓

Towering cliffs

lonesome Pine

Boulders

Brigands' lair

Me!

← Sleigh tracks

Corral

Hoof prints

that window, I might find out where Mamuk was being kept – and where the barbarous brigands had stashed my precious rucksack!

A Helping Antler!

Sliding silently off the boulders, and keeping out of sight of the lookout, I snuck along the back of the corral. The reindeer became restless, blowing great billows of steam from their nostrils and anxiously pawing the ground.

'Shh!' I whispered. I didn't want the brigand to overhear; if they caught me, heaven knows what would happen! 'Good boy, nice reindeer,' I cooed as the largest one stuck his great head through the bars and gently butted me. I stroked his nose and the friendly animal closed his eyes and licked my hand with his long rough tongue.

He was a magnificent bull, standing a good two metres at the shoulder, with a long coat of rich reddish-brown fur. His antlers sprouted from his proud head like great leafless bushes.

Reaching into my pocket, I took out one of the nuts I'd collected in the swamp, and offered it to him. With a grateful nudge he took it from my outstretched palm and I tickled him between his massive antlers.

I stared up at the high open window. The cabin's side offered little in the way of footholds and I knew I wouldn't be able to scale it without rousing the brigands inside. It might be different if I'd had my rucksack of goodies, but without it I was going to need some help.

I climbed into the corral. The big bull reindeer nudged my side, trying to stick his muzzle into my pocket to see if I had any more snacks. I took out the few remaining nuts and coaxed him over to the cabin wall until he was standing directly below

My route to the brigands' window

the open window.

I scattered the nuts on the ground, and as the reindeer lowered his head to feed, I jumped onto his back. He stood up again, chewing the husks contentedly, and I started climbing up his neck and into his velvet-covered antlers. It was as easy as scaling a tree and, standing on tiptoe, I peered through the window into the brigands' hideout.

Eavesdropping Amongst The Eaves

I could hear raised voices and the clinking of mugs in the room below, but it was difficult to see anything – so, hooking my elbows over the sill, I pulled myself up and climbed in through the window. Quietly and carefully I stepped onto a wide, wooden beam.

My old trainers didn't make a sound as I crept along the beam to where I could crouch behind a series of struts that angled up into the shadows of the roof. Directly below me, the noisy robbers sat around a heavy wooden table in the middle of a large, untidy room, congratulating and thumping each other on the back. A battered wood-burning stove stood at one end of the room and two unmade bunk beds were pushed up against a side wall. The floor was littered with clothes, scraps of food, old newspapers and WANTED posters.

At the head of the table sat a man I hadn't seen before – an enormous, scary-looking man with a large round belly and a fleshy face. A plump, wedge-shaped nose protruded from the black mask he wore over his eyes, and a gold ring dangled from one ear. His head was completely bald, but had been decorated with a swirling black tattoo. This was obviously Belcher, the leader of the band of brigands, and he looked very mean.

He's got piggy little eyes just like a truffler! Belcher Boss of the brigands

'Not bad, lads. Not bad at all,' he said in a rich, fruity voice, and thumped the table with his fist. 'Let's see what we've got here, then we'll talk about the reindeer herder.' He sorted through a small pile of coins and wallets, silk handkerchiefs and pocket watches. Picking up a watch, he bit down on it. 'Very good – that's eighteen-carat gold or I'm the son of a mean, bushwhacking bandolero.'

'Ay carumba! You *are* ze son of a mean, bushwhackin' bandolero, boss,' said the brigand with the heavy accent.

'So I am, Ramon.' He grinned. 'Now what have we here?' He pulled my rucksack towards him and tipped out the contents onto the table. 'Did you steal this, Sidekick?' he asked, looking at my explorer's kit with disgust.

'Shucks, no, boss, that was Emmett's haul,' said the other brigand. He was a long lanky youth

Sidekick

with long lank hair and a permanent look of surprise on his face. 'He's done real good again, ain't he? Hee-hee!'

'Emmett!' yelled the boss. 'Get your worthless carcass in 'ere.'

The door opened and the brigand who'd robbed me came nervously inside.

'Is there something wrong, boss?'

'What do you call this? A ball of string, a bottle of water, an animal skull! This junk's no good to us, you nincompoop!'

'Sorry, boss, but it was a particularly slow morning. I only met one kid and that's all he had on him. There's a good hunting knife there, boss. If you don't want it, perhaps I could keep it.'

'Hands off!' yelled Belcher, slipping my knife into his belt. 'I could do with a new dagger. Put all this stuff in the safe and I'll decide what to do with it later. Now I want to talk about the biggest prize of the day: our reindeer herder!'

How on earth am I going to retrieve my rucksack from a safe? I wondered. *And why does Belcher think Mamuk is such a good catch?*

I Drop In On The Conversation!

'We recognizing him, boss. Mamuk's ze leader of zat moth-eaten tribe of reindeer herders out on ze tundra. We thought he might have ze money stashed somewhere,' said Ramon. 'If he has, you're ze man to find out.'

'Oh, I'm sure of it, boys,' said Belcher with a satisfied grin on his greasy face. 'A little bird told me that our dog-eared friend Mamuk and his tribe have got some *great* treasure hidden up in the Snowy Mountains. No one knows where, but it will be my pleasure to try and *squeeze* the information out of 'im.' And the blubbery baron of the brigands cracked his knuckles in anticipation.

'Then what do we do, boss?' asked Emmett.

'Why, then we go and get it, you dunderhead,' said Belcher. 'What do you think we're going to do – offer him a lift home?'

'I just thought, boss, that instead of us going trekking up into the desolate Snowy Mountains for who knows how long, we could get Mamuk's friends to bring the treasure to us.'

'And how are we going to do that, stupid? Write them a letter askin' them, if they would be so kind, to drop the treasure off here?'

'That's right, boss,' said Emmett, looking rather pleased with himself, and the other brigands bellowed with laughter.

'Ay carumba! What a tweet!' guffawed Ramon.

'What I mean is, we send them a ransom note *demanding* the treasure or they'll never see their leader again,' Emmett continued.

Belcher stared at Emmett in amazement, unable to speak for a moment. 'A ransom note?' he said eventually.

'A ransom note, boss.'

'Billowing blizzards! That's one of the best ideas I've ever had!'

'Good thinking, boss,' said Ramon and Sidekick.

'Yeah, good thinking,' sighed Emmett.

'Just a minute, though. How are we goin' to post the letter if we don't know where Mamuk's hideout is?' asked boss Belcher, knitting his brow in concentration.

'Why, we put the note in the saddlebag of one of the reindeers and set the creature free. It's bound to head straight for home.'

'Exactly what I thought,' boasted Belcher. 'Though I'd be happier if someone went with the deer to make sure it arrives. I don't want to be waitin' here for a week to find out the note got lost on the way. Any volunteers?'

No one uttered a word. 'I'll ask again. Any volunteers – Emmett?' said Belcher in a low growl.

'Oh, boss,' complained Emmett. 'Why is it always me?'

It was then that my trainer slipped in the dust on the beam, and with a yell I dropped from the roof and crashed onto the brigands' table.

'*Oof!*' I gasped, bouncing on the springy planks.

'What's going on?' yelled Belcher, jumping to his feet – and I must say he was very quick for such a big man. He grabbed me by the lapels and pulled me towards him.

'Who are you and what are you doing here, you little blighter?' snarled the brigand boss in his rough, fruity tones.

'I, er, rucksack—' I started to say, but Belcher was choking me with his massive fist. '*Eergh!*'

'Come on, speak up, boy, or I'll squeeze the life out of you like the juice from an orange.'

'I don't think he can speak, boss,' said Emmett. 'You're gripping him rather too tightly.'

'Is that so?' said the boss, easing his grip just a little. 'Now then, let's have some answers.'

'This is the kid I robbed,' interrupted Emmett. 'He must have followed us here.'

'And now he knows our plans,' growled Belcher, turning so red I thought his big bald head was going to explode. 'I've a good mind to slice you into strips and feed you to the buzzards.'

'Or,' said Emmett, coughing politely, 'we could get *him* to take the ransom note.'

'And why would he do that?' demanded Belcher.

'Well, he seems mighty attached to that rucksack of his. He told me it was full of vital equipment and he's gone to all the trouble of following us here to try and get it back,' reasoned Emmett. 'Perhaps if we promise to return his rucksack, he'll do this little chore for us.'

Belcher continued to squeeze my neck, staring angrily into my eyes, but gradually he relaxed and then released me. I dropped to the table, gasping for breath. 'Just what I was about to suggest,' he said. 'What do you say, squirt?'

'OK,' I croaked. I didn't seem to have a great deal of choice.

'Right answer, or you would have been used as fuel for the stove,' said boss Belcher. 'Ramon, put him in the lean-to with the reindeer herder while I write the ransom note. Sidekick, put the stew on to warm – I'm as hungry as a wolf after all this thinking.'

Meeting Mamuk

Ramon led me outside into the bright early afternoon. Although the sun was shining, there were still flurries of snow in the chilly air, and at the far end of Frostbite Pass I could see a bank of khaki-coloured clouds gathering in the sky.

'Zere's a big fall of snow on ze way. Looks like you're gonna have ze cold journey, pipsqueak,' said Ramon as he unlocked the door of a small outhouse built onto the side of the main cabin. The brigand shoved me inside and I stumbled across the floor, crashing into the reindeer herder. 'Don't go anywhere,' chuckled Ramon, locking the door and plunging the small shed into gloom.

'Sorry, Mamuk,' I said to the reindeer herder as I picked myself up from the floor. He was surprisingly short, no taller than me, but I couldn't see him properly as his hairy-fringed hood cast a deep shadow over his face; it was as if I was chatting to a headless hooded ghost. It was really eerie!

'What's happening? Who are you?' asked the headless hood.

'I'm Charlie Small. I've been trying to find you, Mamuk. I saw the brigands take you prisoner; they'd just robbed me as well, so I followed them here to try and get my rucksack back and rescue you. Unfortunately the big buffoons caught me.'

It was really eerie

'Why were you looking for me?'

'The tree people said you might be able to show me where my friend Jakeman's factory is,' I explained. 'Although I would have tried to rescue you anyway, honest.'

'And why do you want to go to Jakeman's factory?'

'He's an old pal of mine and I've arranged

to meet him there. He's going to show me how to get back home. Look, he gave me this map.' I took out Jakeman's crumpled map from between the pages of this journal and handed it to the suspicious reindeer herder.

'Really?' said Mamuk, taking the map and folding back his hood so I could see him properly at last. Studying the map, his narrow, friendly eyes creased as a broad grin spread across his oval face, and his long pointed beard vibrated as he started chuckling to himself. 'Ho, ho! Sure, I know old Jakeman. He's a funny old chap, but a very clever inventor. I *can* show you the way, Charlie, but first,' he added, getting serious again, 'we've got to get out of this dreadful jam. Do you know what these beastly brigands want from me?'

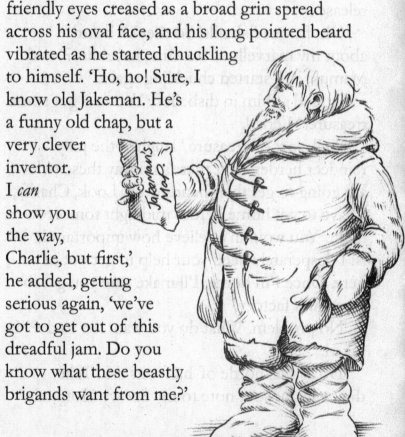

'Treasure,' I said, although looking at the man's scruffy clothes it seemed silly to suggest he had any money at all, let alone a pile of fabulous treasure. 'I know it's daft, but Belcher thinks you've got a fortune stashed away in the Snowy Mountains. The brigands want me to deliver a ransom note to your people, demanding this treasure hoard in return for your release.'

'Oh, frozen fishtails! So they've heard about my marvellous treasure, have they?' said Mamuk, and started chuckling again.

I stared at him in disbelief. 'You *have* got some treasure?' I cried.

'Well, sort of treasure,' laughed the jolly reindeer herder. 'But there's no way these twits are going to get their hands on it. Look, Charlie, I have to get home before midnight tomorrow night. You wouldn't believe how important it is! I desperately need your help to get out of here. Once I'm home, I'll make sure you get to Jakeman's factory.'

'No problem. What do you want me to do?' I asked.

'Do as this horde of half-wits ask. Take their silly ransom note to my Snowy Mountain hideout; Rudy will show you the way.'

'Who's Rudy?'

'The leader of my reindeer team. He's the biggest, strongest and fastest reindeer in the whole of the Frozen North. When you get there, ask for Arnuq and give her my password – it will prove that I trust you,' said Mamuk.

'OK,' I said, starting to get excited. 'What is it?'

'What's what?' asked Mamuk.

'The password!'

'Ho, ho! Of course! The password is: *The reindeer fly at midnight!*'

'*The reindeer fly at midnight,*' I repeated.

'You have it exactly.' The reindeer herder smiled. 'Tell Arnuq what's happened; she'll know what to do. She *must* get me out of here straight away.'

'But once the ransom has been paid, the brigands will release you anyway,' I said.

'Ho, ho! You don't really believe that, do you?' said Mamuk, chuckling to himself. 'You can't trust those sneaky snakes, Charlie. Anyway, once they find out what my treasure really is, I wouldn't be surprised if they don't string me up from the nearest gibbet.'

'Why? What is your fabulous treasure?'

'Oh, you'll see when you get to my hideout. Just try and make sure Arnuq's here before midnight tomorrow.'

'What's so important about tomorrow night?' I asked.

'Frozen fishtails! Don't you know the date? Can't you guess who I am? Ho, ho! If the brigands knew, they would be demanding treasure from every household in the land!'

'I've no idea what the date is, but I know you're Mamuk, leader of the reindeer herders.'

'Yes, Charlie, but I'm also known as—'

Just then the outhouse door burst open. Sidekick was standing there.

'Come on, maggot, the boss is ready for you,' he said, ushering me outside.

'Good luck, Charlie,' said Mamuk. 'Don't forget—'

But Sidekick slammed the door shut and I didn't hear any more.

A Reindeer Ride To The Snowy Mountains ▲▲▲

Sidekick bundled me back into the cabin,

where the brigand Belcher
sprawled in his great carved
chair. He handed me a
folded piece of paper.

'Take this to Mamuk's
people. Tell 'em we mean
business. If they don't do as the note says, we
will bury their chief so deep in the snow they'll
never find him, and his blood will turn to slush
in his veins. Hee, hee!'

'What about my rucksack?' I asked.

'It will be waiting for you at the lonesome
pine. You must take the treasure there. Any
funny business and the smelly old herder will get
it, your scabby old rucksack will be destroyed
and I'll hunt you down and slice you in two.
Understood?'

'Understood,' I gulped.

'Good. Now eat some of this,
squirt. You have a long journey ahead
of you and we don't want you fainting
from hunger on the way.' Belcher handed
me a bowl of the brigands' bubbling
stew and I wolfed it down. It was rich,
tangy and delicious, and warmed me
up right down to my frosty toes.

Lovely stew!

As soon as I'd finished, the brigands gave me a thick coat of animal hide to wear and I was taken outside to the corral.

'Take one of the reindeer,' demanded Belcher. 'They are bound to know their way back to Mamuk's place. And remember; any funny business and I'll start slitting gizzards – and yours will be one of 'em.'

'I'll take this one,' I said, climbing onto the fence rails and then jumping onto the back of the biggest reindeer. It was the same animal I'd used to climb up to the window; from Mamuk's description I was sure it must be Rudy.

'Whatever,' said Belcher, opening the corral gate.

I grabbed hold of Rudy's antlers as he trotted out of the compound with a shake of his proud head.

'Now *go!*' yelled the brigand boss, giving Rudy a mighty slap on the rump. The reindeer leaped forward and, with a bellow, raced out across the snow.

'Home, Rudy,' I yelled, hanging on for dear life. 'Take me to your home!'

The snorting reindeer was much easier to ride

than the swamp hopper and I didn't have to bother trying to steer – he obviously knew where he was going. Up the slope of the pass we galloped, down the narrow gulch and into the pine forest. Without faltering or slowing, Rudy raced out into the wide snowy valley where I'd been robbed, and up a steep, narrow path that climbed the cliffs on the far side.

As we reached the top and dashed across a frosty, flat, treeless plain covered in a thick blanket of moss, the yellow clouds banked and swirled above us, and the snow started to fall again. Great flakes as big as saucers dropped from the sky, hitting me in the face with wet slaps and stinging my cheeks. Brrr, it was cold! I was glad I was wearing a thick fur coat.

Rudy lowered his head and increased his speed; jets of steam blasted from his nostrils into the freezing air. I held on tighter, frightened I was going to slip from his shaggy back, but soon I was so cold, my hands had frozen around his antlers as securely as if they had been welded on, and not even a hurricane could have dislodged me!

My teeth were chattering and a long icicle had formed on the end of my nose. As we careered

Yee-hah!

across the tundra, the sky started to darken. *How much longer is this ride going to last?* I wondered. *Soon it will be night-time, and then it will get* really *cold!* Even as this thought crossed my mind, the sun disappeared below the horizon and the landscape was plunged into sudden darkness.

Our journey went on. I couldn't see much of our surroundings, but I soon became aware we were starting to climb. I could hear loose rocks clattering under Rudy's feet and then silence as he ploughed into a deep bed of snow. I could make out the silhouettes of huge peaks against the dark velvet sky and I knew we must be in the Snowy Mountains at last.

Without putting a foot wrong, Rudy climbed the craggy paths, leaping across sheer gaps where the mountainside had collapsed and jumping from rock to rock as we raced up almost vertically.

Finally Rudy started to slow down, first to a canter and then a trot. Now I could see we were following a path that dropped away to nothing on one side; on the other, a series of cave mouths gaped in the mountainside. All of a sudden the reindeer darted inside one of the caves and followed it deep inside the snow-covered peak. The dark and gloomy cave came to an end at a featureless rock wall; Rudy stopped and, lifting his head, bellowed three times.

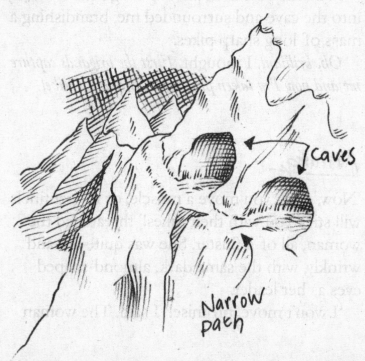

caves

Narrow path

A strange humming noise came from beyond the cave wall, reminding me of the wonderful glow bugs I'd met in the Underworld. Then, with a whooshing noise like a lorry's airbrakes, a hidden door opened up in the wall, throwing a wedge of light across the floor. A short woman, dressed in the same sort of garb as Mamuk, stepped into the cave. She took one look at me and started to shout:

'Sentinels, we have an intruder! Come quickly! Sentinels!'

A dozen little men piled through the doorway into the cave and surrounded me, brandishing a mass of long sharp pikes.

Oh, brilliant, I thought. *First the brigands capture me and now I'm taken prisoner by Mamuk's tribe!*

Arnuq

'Now, don't you move a muscle, or my sentinels will stick you with their pikes!' threatened the woman, all of a fluster. She was quite old and wrinkly, with the same dark, almond-shaped eyes as her leader.

'I won't move, promise!' I said. The woman

might be old and
rather nervous, but
she looked quite
determined.

'Right,' she
said. 'Who are
you? How come
you're riding
our Rudy, and
where on earth
is Mamuk?'

'My name is
Charlie Small and I've
come to deliver this,' I said, unclasping my
frozen fingers from Rudy's antlers to rummage
in my pocket for the ransom note. 'I was told to
give this note to someone called Arnuq. A band
of brigands are holding Mamuk prisoner and
want your hoard of treasure in exchange for his
release.'

'I'm Arnuq,' said the woman severely,
snatching the note from my hand. She unfolded
it and read the contents carefully. From my perch
on Rudy's back I could see the ransom note quite
clearly. The writing was very bad and Belcher's
spelling was atrocious! This is what it said:

To the Raindeer peeple
of the Northurn Tundra,

We are holding Mamuk prisna.
We will freeeze him into a
humun lollipop if you don't do
exacktlee as We say.

We want yor fabulus tresha!
Take it to the lownsum pine
at the hed of Frostbite Pass
tomorrow, 6.00 p.m. sharp. No
funnee bizness or Mamuk gets
it!

Yours trooly,

Belcher

Boss of the Barbarous Brigands

'What on earth makes you think we've got any treasure?' asked Arnuq, frowning at me.

'It's not me, it's the brigands!' I cried.

'How do I know *you're* not a brigand?' she snapped. 'You sure look like one. Why shouldn't I lock you up somewhere and throw away the key?'

And the sentinels started poking me with their pikes. 'Brigand! Brigand!' they chanted.

'Ouch!' I cried, beginning to panic. 'Leave off.' I was starting to think I would have been better off staying with the brigands! Then I remembered Mamuk's password. *'The reindeer fly at midnight!'* I cried. 'Mamuk said to tell you, *the reindeer fly at midnight!'*

pikes

'Well, why didn't you say so, Charlie?' said Arnuq with a big, beaming smile. 'Now I know you are Mamuk's friend. Come on then,' she said, clapping her hands just like my gran does to hurry me along. 'We must get ready to go and rescue Mamuk.'

'Mamuk said we mustn't believe the brigands. He doesn't think they will release him even after they've got the treasure,' I warned.

'No, my dear! It's not very likely at all, seeing as we don't have any! I'm afraid we must be prepared to fight for Mamuk's release.'

Fight! I thought. This was a bit worrying; nobody told me I might have to fight!

'But Mamuk told me you *did* have a sort of treasure,' I gasped.

'A sort of treasure, yes; but not one a bunch of bloodthirsty brigands will be happy with,' said Arnuq. 'Hurry along, dear, and I'll show you.' And again she clapped her hands.

With great difficulty I slid down off Rudy's back. On stiff legs I followed Arnuq and the sentinels through the stone door and down a passage lit by a long line of flickering candles. At the far end was another door, which the sentinels heaved open, and I walked out onto a stone platform that looked down into a large chamber. The scene below took my breath away.

'Welcome to our fabulous grotto,' said Arnuq.

The Marvellous Grotto

The chamber was packed with machines of all

sizes, shapes and colours, and their clanking, banging and hissing filled the air. Everywhere, Mamuk's fur-clad people were scurrying about, pulling levers, carrying boxes and adjusting dials.

'What are they doing? What are they making?' I asked. Then, as my eyes started to make sense of the confusion below, I gasped again. 'Toys,' I said. 'They're making toys!'

Each machine was sending out a line of different playthings. There were game consoles, dolls, scooters and skateboards; bicycles, books, globes and train sets. Anything you've ever wished for or desired was popping out of one machine or another. I couldn't believe it!

'Yes, dear.' Arnuq grinned. 'And that's our great treasure. I don't think the brigands will be happy with that, do you?'

'Not likely; I imagine they're expecting a pile of gold,' I said. I could just see the robbers eagerly opening a treasure chest only to find it full of dolls and selection boxes. They wouldn't be very impressed! 'But why are you making all these toys?'

'For tomorrow night, silly,' said Arnuk, clasping her hands together and staring down at the grotto of goodies with bright, darting eyes.

Bicycle wheels

Board games

Teddy bears

'What's so important about tomorrow night? Mamuk kept on about it too.'

'Oh, Charlie,' said Arnuq; she waddled over to a huge pinboard, took down a calendar and handed it to me. 'That's tomorrow night. Doesn't it ring any bells, my dear?'

I stared at the date Arnuq's finger was pointing at. 'The twenty-fourth of December,' I cried. 'It's Christmas Eve! But why is it so important to Mamuk?'

Arnuq looked at me, but didn't say a word. I gazed down at the manic activity going on in the grotto and my head buzzed in confusion. Then it came to me. *Oh, Charlie, you fool! Of course: reindeer and sleighs, toys and Christmas Eve. Bloomin' heck!*

'That means Mamuk must be—'

'Ssh!' said Arnuq, putting a finger up to her lips. 'Now you know why it's so important he's released before midnight tomorrow.'

'You bet!' I cried. I couldn't believe it; I was going on a mission to try and save Christmas for every boy and girl in the world. It was the most important assignment ever, and now I *was* prepared to fight to try and free Mamuk!

'The brigands won't be happy if we turn up

with a sleigh full of teddy bears, though,' said
Arnuq. 'And if we turn up with nothing, we'll be
in real trouble.'

'So what are we going to do?'

'Let's go and look down there, dear; we might
get a flash of inspiration!'

Treasure In The Grotto

Arnuq and I clambered down a flight of
metal steps into the grotto below. The noise
grew louder and louder, until we had to shout
above the clanking of gears and pistons and
the tooting of whistles. I walked past rows of
machinery painted in bright harlequin patterns,
and wove through crowds of hurrying workers.
I gazed at the glut of incredible playthings and
wondered how they could be used as a ransom
treasure.

I passed roller-blades, trampolines, spinning
tops and radio-controlled planes – fantastic
stuff, but I think the brigands were more
interested in cold, hard cash, and lots of it!
Then I saw something that gave me an idea!

One of the machines was pumping out boiled

sweets, candy canes, gobstoppers and humbugs in every colour of the rainbow. As they dropped from a spiralling glass tube into little striped boxes on a conveyor belt, they shone like lumps of pure crystal. By the side of the machine a worker was turning a wheel, and as he did so, the shape of the sweets changed.

Jakeman's Boiled Sweet maker

I rushed over and watched more closely. Imagine my surprise when I saw a small oval badge on the machine that read:

JAKEMAN'S
BOILED SWEET MAKER
SPECIAL EDITION
MIXES, COOKS AND SHAPES!
*

Good old Jakeman, I thought. *His mechanical marvels get everywhere!*

'Can it make diamond-shaped sweets?' I asked.

'Of course; any shape you like,' said the candy maker, and turned the dial to number four. Immediately the shape of the sweets changed and a line of perfect, diamond-cut pastilles dropped from the tube. They looked like deep red rubies, rich green emeralds and shiny bright sapphires.

'There's our treasure!' I said to Arnuq.

'Perfect.' She smiled. 'We can add some of these as well, and she reached into a deep bin beside another machine and scooped out an armful of big golden coins. 'Chocolate!' she said, and burst out laughing.

Before long she had got one of the helpers to paint a large wooden toy-box to look like a treasure chest and we filled it with our goodies. Then Arnuq led me over to a rack of black tubes that looked a bit like drainpipes.

'We should take some of these along, Charlie, in case there's any trouble,' she said.

'What are they?'

'Well, they're toys really, but they might come in useful. They're for extreme snowballing; we call them snow bazookas! Here, have a go.'

She murmured something to a young helper, and clapped her hands impatiently as he rushed up the steps and out through the stone door. He soon returned, carrying a bucket of fresh snow.

Taking one of the pipes from the rack, Arnuq placed it on my shoulder. Then, sliding back a hatch in the tube, she filled a compartment with some of the snow.

'See if you can hit that big teddy on the shelf over there, dear. Take aim through this,' she said, and flipped down a sight, similar to the one on the swamp hopper. I took careful aim and pulled a trigger under the tube.

BOOF! A ball of snow shot from the bazooka at a hundred miles an hour and the poor teddy flew off the shelf in an explosion of snow and landed at the far side of the grotto.

'They take six rounds. What do you think?' asked Arnuq.

'Perfect!' I grinned.

A Quick Snooze

Everything is ready for the task ahead. It's already dawn; Arnuq has loaded the treasure chest onto the back of a racing sleigh, and Rudy and another reindeer are standing by to take us. I was surprised to learn that only Arnuq and I would be going on the rescue mission.

'Why don't we take the sentinels or an army of helpers with us? We could overrun the brigands much more easily then.'

'The sentinels must stay and guard the mountain, and the others are much too busy – they only have one day left to finish making up their orders. No, we must go alone. Don't worry though, Charlie – we'll be fine. We must be able to outwit a band of barbarous brigands, surely!'

I didn't feel so confident; wasn't Arnuq a bit old and nervy to be going on a dangerous rescue mission?

She must have guessed what I was thinking, for she smiled and said, 'Don't worry, dear. I'm a lot tougher than I look. I used to be the tribe's champion walrus hunter.'

Yes, I thought, *but how long ago was that?*

Now I'm in a part of the mountain where Mamuk and his people live. Arnuq insisted I get some sleep before we started back, and I must say I feel absolutely shattered. In a chamber adjacent to the toy grotto, a whole city of apartments has been built into the rock. Layers of balconies rise up from the chamber floor, all reached by tubular glass lifts. I'm in bed in a room on the very top floor, wrapped in a thick fur blanket.

I've been busy writing up these latest incredible adventures in my journal, but now I must get some shut-eye; I'm whacked out, and tomorrow Arnuq and I are going to try and save Christmas!

Take-Off!

It was late morning by the time I'd got up and had my breakfast; we were in a hurry.

'Feeling rested?' asked Arnuq. 'Good, then let's go.' She led me to one of the glass lifts, which took us down, down, down, to the very base of the mountain, where we stepped out into another vast room.

'This is the launching chamber,' she explained, and pointed to where Rudy and his companion were already harnessed to the racing sleigh, chomping at their bits and pawing the ground in anticipation. Ahead of them gaped the mouth of a low tunnel.

The sleigh was fantastic; it looked like a racing car, sleek and low and shaped like a missile. I

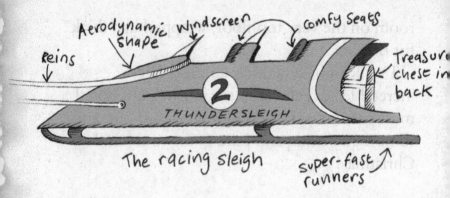

Reins

Aerodynamic shape

Windscreen

comfy seats

Treasure chest in back

2

THUNDERSLEIGH

The racing sleigh

super-fast runners

waited as Arnuq took a large circular hunting horn from a hook on the wall.

'What's that for?' I enquired.

'Oh, just in case of trouble, dear,' she answered mysteriously, checking the treasure chest on the back of the sleigh and stashing the loaded bazookas down the side. She stepped into the driver's seat and I climbed in behind her.

'Put your safety belt on, Charlie. We don't want any accidents,' Arnuq called over her shoulder, and I clipped my belt buckles together. Then, with a crack of her whip, she cried, 'On, Rudy. On, Donner!' and we took off like a bullet from a gun.

'*Aargh!*' I yelled as we zoomed at breathtaking speed into the low tunnel and along its super-smooth ice floor; the sides of the tunnel whipped past my ears in a blur. '*Yikes!*' I screamed as the floor started to slope up towards the exit, and '*Whoa!*' I gulped as we shot from the mountain in a wide, flying arc.

'We're flying!' I yelled. 'I'm actually flying in a sleigh. Yippee!' Then, with a bump and a bang, we hit the ground again and shot along a wide track that led us between the lofty peaks.

'Oh, I thought we'd taken off then,' I gasped, trying to get my breath back. 'I thought these reindeer might be able to fly!'

'Actually, that *is* our take-off ramp,' said Arnuq with a grin. 'Mamuk's herd *can* fly – otherwise we'd never get our work done – but not until midnight on Christmas Eve. That's when the magic starts!'

With a flick of the reins she urged on Rudy and Donner, and we blasted through the mountain range and off towards the tundra.

Rendezvous At The Lonesome Pine

It was already six o'clock in the evening when Rudy guided the racing sleigh into the narrow opening of Frostbite Pass. We rattled at full speed along the winding gorge until it opened out and we could see the lonesome pine in front of us and tendrils of smoke from the brigands' cabin, way down the snow-covered slope. Arnuq pulled the sleigh to a halt a little way from the tree.

As we stepped out, three figures emerged from behind the pine: Belcher, Ramon – and yes, there was the short figure of Mamuk, the hood of his coat completely concealing his face. I was surprised: the brigands had kept to their side of the bargain. I only hoped our confectionery treasure would fool them long enough for us to make our getaway. Both Belcher and Ramon held their pistols at the ready, though for the moment they were pointed to the ground.

'You've cut it a bit fine,' growled Belcher, looking at an ornate pocket watch. 'Here's your beloved leader; have you got our treasure?'

'We have it in the back of the sleigh,' said Arnuq nervously, looking small and vulnerable in comparison to the big brigand boss. Again I wondered if she was up to this rescue mission.

'Then drag it out and let's have a look,' said Belcher greedily. 'And no tricks or I'll blast the

hairy herder into the middle of next week!' He
levelled his pistol at the small figure by his side.
Mamuk showed no signs of nervousness, but
stood there stock-still.

We unloaded the heavy chest. It looked
just the job as we dragged it to the middle of
the space between our sleigh and the waiting
brigands.

'Lift the lid and let's
see what you've
brought. If I
think there's
enough loot,
we'll make the
exchange.'

I lifted the lid of
our toy-box and the
pile of sweets and
foil-covered chocolate
coins glowed in the
evening light. Belcher stepped forward eagerly,
his eyes nearly popping out of his head at the
sight of the longed-for treasure.

'Right, take a few steps back,' he said. 'Go on,
further. I don't trust you an inch. OK, that'll do.'
He ran towards the chest, fell to his knees and

feasted his eyes on the sparkling contents.

He put a hand in and scooped up some raspberry-flavoured rubies. 'Luverlee!' he cried. 'OK, you can go now.' He waved his pistol, dismissing us. 'Go on, get lost. Vamoose!'

'What about Mamuk? We won't leave without him, you know,' said Arnuq, wringing her hands and edging towards the sleigh.

'Yeah, and where's my rucksack . . . ? Hold on, what's happening?'

The short figure of Mamuk had started to grow, and as he did so, he pulled back his hood and let the coat fall to the ground. It wasn't Mamuk at all; it was Sidekick. He'd been squatting on his haunches inside Mamuk's big hide coat. What a dirty trick!

'You treacherous tricksters!' I cried. 'That's not fair!'

'What did you expect?' sniggered Belcher, picking up some coins and letting them cascade back into the chest. 'We are brigands, you know! We've decided to keep Mamuk a bit longer; our hideout needs a good spring-clean and I'm sure there are a million other little jobs we could get him to do. Anyway, once we've spent this little lot, we might be asking you for more!'

''Scuse me, boss,' interrupted Sidekick, 'but they're not very clinky.'

'What are you blathering about?' asked Belcher with an exasperated tut.

'The coins – they're not very clinky, boss.'

Belcher froze, and with a frown on his fat, glowering face he picked up a coin and tested it between his teeth.

'Oh, lumme! We're for it. Get the bazookas,' Arnuq whispered to me.

'*Ptah!*' roared Belcher as I reached into the sleigh. 'They're bloomin' chocolate!'

'Ooh, lovely; I like chocolate,' said Sidekick, delving into the chest.

'This treasure is fake; *you're* the treacherous tricksters,' bellowed Belcher.

'Not so nice when the boot's on the other foot, is it?' I cried, and as the

They're bloomin' chocolate!

brigand boss levelled his pistol at me, I swung the snow bazooka up from the sleigh and fired from the hip.

BOOF! The ball of snow exploded on Belcher's hand and his pistol went spinning through the air and fell into the thick snow. The brigand dived to the ground, cursing as he sifted through the drift for his gun. Arnuq fired her bazooka: *BOOF!* Ramon was knocked clean off his feet and sent crashing into the trunk of the lonesome pine, where he slid to the ground in a daze! Brilliant – Arnuq was a crack shot!

BOOF! I caught Sidekick in the tummy as he leaned over the chest, greedily stuffing chocolate coins into his mouth. The snowball lifted him into the air and sent him rolling head over heels down the slope!

'Back in the sleigh!' yelled Arnuq. 'Go, Rudy, go, Donner!'

We leaped into the already moving sleigh as the brigands got to their feet and made for their horses.

'Head towards the rise over there,' I yelled, pointing towards the cliff-tops on the far side of the pass, which were covered in thick drifts of snow. 'I've got an idea!'

'OK, Charlie,' said Arnuq, flicking the reins. 'Go, boys, go!'

Snowfalls And Snowballs! #☺

Rudy and Donner belted along the snow-covered ground below the steep sides of the pass.

'Time to call in the reserves,' cried Arnuq, and blew a long mournful note on her hunting horn.

I looked around to see if hordes of herders were going to come swarming magically into the pass – but nothing happened at all! I was just about to ask what exactly *was* supposed to happen when I became aware of the muffled hooves of the brigands' horses; as we approached the foot of the snowy cliff-tops I'd seen, they were only a couple of hundred metres behind us. I fired off a couple of volleys at our charging pursuers.

'Just here,' I yelled, and Arnuq pulled up the deer beyond the snow-laden cliffs. I rolled off the sleigh, clutching my snow bazooka. 'Try and keep me covered,' I cried, loading the tube with fresh ammo.

Arnuq dived to the ground by my side and started firing volleys of snowballs at the approaching brigands. She was fantastic – I could quite believe she was the best walrus hunter in the tribe!

Boof! Boof! Boof! She fired again and again and the brigands skidded to a halt and flung themselves to the ground behind a ridge of snow at the base of the cliffs. *Ptang!* They started firing their flintlocks. Luckily the pistols only carried one round and it took them a little while to reload.

Boof! Arnuq fired again. *Ptang!* came the brigands' reply, but as they stopped to refill their weapons, I stepped out from behind our shelter, aimed my bazooka at the top of the cliff, and fired.

'Ha ha! That was a little wide,' yelled Belcher, and *ptang!* he fired again.

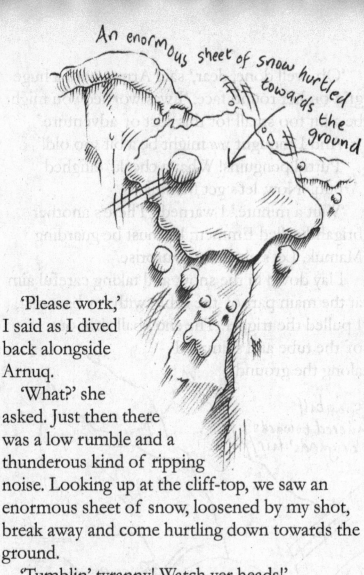

An enormous sheet of snow hurtled towards the ground

'Please work,'
I said as I dived
back alongside
Arnuq.

'What?' she
asked. Just then there
was a low rumble and a
thunderous kind of ripping
noise. Looking up at the cliff-top, we saw an
enormous sheet of snow, loosened by my shot,
break away and come hurtling down towards the
ground.

'Tumblin' tyranny! Watch yer heads!'
screamed the brigands, but it was too late; with
a mighty *crump!* they were buried under the
avalanche!

'Oh, well done, dear,' said Arnuq with a huge grin on her round face. 'I was worried you might be a bit too small for this sort of adventure.'

'And I thought *you* might be a bit too old!'

'Putrid penguins! What a cheek!' laughed Arnuq. 'Now, let's get Mamuk.'

'Wait a minute,' I warned. 'There's another brigand called Emmett; he must be guarding Mamuk. Let's give him a surprise.'

I lay down in the snow, and taking careful aim at the main part of the cabin with my bazooka, I pulled the trigger. The snowball shot out of the tube and skimmed along the ground.

My snowball thundered towards the brigands' lair!

Rumble!!

As it rolled at breakneck speed down the long slope towards the brigands' hideout, it picked up more and more snow, growing larger and larger. Soon it was the size of a beach ball, then a large boulder. By the time it reached the cabin, rumbling along the ground like Jakeman's mighty mole, it was as big as a hot-air balloon!

Whump! It hit the hideout square on, and with a sound of cracking and splintering wood it smashed through the front wall. *Crash!* The snowball came to a stop, piling up against the back wall as the roof creaked and started to sag. My aim had been true – the only parts of the building left undamaged were the corral and the lean-to where Mamuk was imprisoned.

'Wow!' gulped Arnuq. 'Was that supposed to happen?'

'Well, I thought it might break down the front door,' I admitted.

'It's certainly done that, dear.' Arnuq smiled, and we burst out laughing. Just then we heard some groans from the avalanche of snow and, glancing over, we saw that Belcher and his pals were starting to crawl out from underneath.

'Let's go!' I yelled, and as the light began to fade from the sky, we leaped back onto our racing sleigh and made a dash for the cabin. As we pulled up outside, we could see Emmett's boots sticking out from under the pile of snow in the wreckage, wriggling and kicking in fury.

'I say, is anybody there?' came his muffled call. 'Help! Someone get me out!'

'This way,' I said to Arnuq, ignoring the struggling bandit, and led her round the side of the cabin to the outhouse. 'Stand back, Mamuk,' I yelled, and with one blast from my bazooka, the door burst open.

The reindeer herder emerged from the hut, smiling and punching the air in delight. 'Ho, ho! Well done. I knew I could rely on you two,' he said. 'And we still have time to get home and load up for our journey,' he added, looking at his watch.

But our fun wasn't over yet. We heard a yell from the other side of the pass: the brigands had extricated themselves from the snow and were already galloping down the slope towards us.

'Oh no! What are we going to do now?' I cried.

Arnuq's Polar Troops

Neither of my friends said anything, but Arnuq put the hunting horn to her lips once more and played a series of clear notes.

'What good will that do?' I asked. 'Nothing happened the last time you blew it.'

'That was just a rallying call,' said Arnuq confidently. She didn't seem in the least bit old or nervous any more. 'This time I blew a call to action.'

Arnuq blew her hunting horn

Even as she spoke, I thought I could see something happening a short distance away to the brigands' left: there was a strange flowing movement, as if the snow itself was stirring. Then, as I looked more closely, I started to make out pairs of beady black eyes here, and great padding paws there. Now I could discern faces with black button noses, and I realized what I was seeing: a group of pure white polar bears was lumbering across the pass to cut off the approaching brigands.

They growled and roared, showing their big pink mouths lined with flesh-ripping teeth. Almost immediately we heard a cry of sheer panic from our attackers; they turned their horses and, furiously spurring them on, galloped away. The big bears shot across the pass, their long fur rippling in the wind, hot on the brigands' heels.

'Come back, fellas! Don't leave me here on my own!' yelled Emmett as he finally crawled out from under the huge snowball. He ran over to his horse and unhitched it from the corral fence. As his steed took off, he swung himself into the saddle and galloped away after his friends.

'Wait for me!' he screamed at his retreating pals, but they didn't take a blind bit of notice!

'Hurrah!' we cheered as the mighty polar army chased the brigands out of Frostbite Pass. 'See the barbarous boneheads off!' I wonder if they escaped?

Ready For Christmas

With the brigands gone, I raced into the cabin to try and find the safe that contained my precious rucksack. *Oh no!* It was lost under the huge pile of snow! I frantically started to dig.

'Frozen fishtails! Come on, Charlie. We've got to go,' said Mamuk.

'I need my explorer's kit. Just hang on a minute – I'm sure I can find it.' But it was no good. The more I dug the more I realized I was fighting a losing battle. It would take a month of Sundays to find.

'Don't worry about your old kitbag, Charlie,' said Mamuk.

'That's easy for you to say,' I cried in a panic.

'Trust me, Charlie, don't worry about it,' he said, his eyes twinkling with good humour. 'Now, let's go. We're already late.'

Sulkily I slid down the snow to where my two companions were waiting, and tried to put the loss out of my mind. We released the rest of Mamuk's reindeer from the corral and hitched them to his sleigh, which we found parked round the back of the ruined cabin. I climbed into Arnuq's racer again, and with much calling and geeing, the two sledges moved off and soon we'd left Frostbite Pass far behind – with my rucksack still in it and *lost for ever*.

By the time we rode into the cave at Mamuk's mountain home, it was nearly midnight. A sentinel waiting by the stone door that led through to the toy factory pushed a projection of rock, and with a low rumble, a wide door slid open in the side of the cave. Mamuk steered his sleigh through the doors and we followed him into a small room. With a bit of nudging and bumping we managed to fit in, and Mamuk pressed a button on a panel in the wall. The room started to hum and shake and I realized we were in a large lift which was taking us down inside the mountain.

When the doors opened again, we emerged into the launching chamber. The whole place was a swarm of activity. Mamuk steered his sleigh over to the take-off track, at the head of a score of other sledges. Each sledge had a team of reindeer harnessed to it and was already piled high with parcels and presents; small herders sat waiting in the driving seats. As a group of helpers loaded his sleigh with goodies and hitched Rudy and Donner to his team, Mamuk beckoned me over.

'Come on, Charlie,' he cried, riffling through a large stack of delivery notes. 'There's no time to lose! It's about to strike midnight and if you want to go to Jakeman's you'd better climb on board. Ho, ho!'

I leaped onto the back of his sleigh and snuggled down amongst the mountains of gifts.

Just then, a big clock at the top of a tall metal gantry began to strike and the reindeer started to grow restless. They shivered and shook and flicked their ears. As the chiming stopped, Mamuk yelled, 'Away!' and his sleigh darted forward and raced into the take-off tunnel. The other sleighs followed close behind.

Rudy and his team leaped from the end of the launch pad – and we took off. This time we didn't come straight back down again; we continued to climb higher and higher, galloping across the moonlit sky. Oh, boy, it was *fantastic*!

I gazed down as the mountains passed by, faster and faster. Soon it seemed as if the whole world was spinning like a top; everything became a crazy blur and my head was starting to whir. I looked behind me: all the other sleighs were fanned out like an aerobatic display team. Then they shot off in different directions and we were alone in a wide black sky.

Now I couldn't see anything above or below me; it was as if we were suspended in the vastness of space. I yawned and closed my eyes. I was very weary and it was an effort to stay awake. *You must stay awake*, I told myself. *You'll never have an adventure like this again.*

Then a thought struck me – a brainwave! If Mamuk really is who I think he is, why can't *he* take me home tonight? Tree said that Mamuk knew where everyone lived – he was bound to go there at some point in his travels! I could skip going to Jakeman's and *be home by morning!* Yes, that's exactly what I would do— Then I fell into a deep, deep sleep.

Here We Go Again!

I opened my eyes to see the sunlight shining through a thin roof of material just above my head. I sat up sharply and looked around. I was in a small one-man tent! *What's going on? I wondered. Where's Mamuk, and why aren't I in the back of his sleigh? I've been abandoned – and I've missed my chance of asking him to drop me off at home! Dash, blow and double darn it!*

Now where was I? I obviously hadn't been delivered to Jakeman's factory like he'd promised. I scrambled forward, opened the tent flap and looked out on a bright, sunny day. A patch of grass stretched out in front of me and then suddenly dropped away. Beyond I could see a beautiful green valley with a wide silver river running along the bottom. On the far side of the river stood a small town with a church and a group of red-roofed houses. Even from this distance I could make out tiny ant-sized figures moving along the streets.

Further down the valley, the river widened into a broad estuary, with countless streams and ditches dividing the land into hundreds of grass-tufted islands. Here were yet more buildings: wharves and docks with a flotilla of ocean-going sailing ships at anchor. Towards the coast, resting on the high ground above the far side of the valley, was a large building; a tall, soot-blackened brick monstrosity, with a series of tall chimneys reaching into the sky and sending out plumes of grey smoke.

Where the heck am I? Why have I been dumped—? Hello, what's this? My knee had knocked against something by the tent flap. Lifting the hide coat on which I'd been lying, I found a parcel wrapped in gaily-coloured paper. A label on the side read:

To Charlie,
HAPPY CHRISTMAS!
love from
Mannuk and 😊
Arnuq xxx

I don't believe it! Mamuk had abandoned me in the middle of nowhere, but he'd left me a present! I ripped off the gift wrap and there, to my astonishment, was a brand new rucksack. Oh no, no, no, Mamuk! I know you said not to worry about my rucksack, but it's what was *in* it that was so important, not the bag itself! Then, as I disconsolately dropped it back on the ground, I heard something clatter inside.

I undid the buckle, tipped the rucksack upside down, and out poured my trusty explorer's kit: my maps and water bottle; my penknife and bat skull; the shark's tooth and useless train ticket; everything that had been in my old bag seemed to be in this one!

Not only that, but there was a new lasso and telescope to replace those I'd lost in the fiery pit in the Underworld. (There was no crocodile tooth, though!) Even Jakeman's map in my pocket had been mysteriously filled in, all the missing areas completed. How had Mamuk done it? This was mind-boggling magic; but then again, he is a very special person indeed, isn't he?

At the bottom of the bag was a folded slip of paper, and this is what it said:

Dear Charlie,

I'm so sorry I have to drop you off here, but I'm in a dreadful hurry. You are fast asleep and I don't want to wake you.

On the other side of the valley, you will find Jakeman's factory. I wonder you didn't ask me to drop you off at your house – what's the address? I might be going that way. My good old pal Jakeman will help you, though, and it's better you find your _own_ way home.

Good luck, Charlie, and thank you so much for helping to save Christmas!

Your good friend

Mamuk

P.S. I hope the explorer's kit is OK!

On To Jakeman's! At last

Well, I thought, at least Mamuk hasn't completely abandoned me. But why is it better for me to find my own way home? Maybe Mamuk thinks it will be character-building or something – and maybe he's right. After all, I *am* having the adventure of a lifetime – a hundred lifetimes, in fact!

Feeling more cheerful, I crawled out of the tent and raised the new telescope to my eye. Yes, Mamuk was right. I could now see that the huge sooty building across the valley had an arched sign above its main gates, and on the sign I could quite clearly make out the words:

JAKEMAN'S FACTORY

Just a short trek and I will be there. Then, *home, here I come!*

I sat in the tent and wrote up my journal, then packed my explorer's kit, and the tent, into the brand-new rucksack. As I threaded my arms through the straps, I noticed a small plastic disc on the right strap, up near my shoulder. On

the disc were five coloured
buttons, one in the middle
with four surrounding it,
like this:

The button pad on my new rucksack.

Hello, I thought, *what can they
be for? My old rucksack certainly
didn't have them.* Cautiously, one by
one, I pressed the four outer buttons on the
disc, but nothing happened. They must be a silly
designer decoration. *That's a bit of a waste of time*,
I thought, and absent-mindedly squeezed the
central button.

WHOOSH! A noise came from under the
rucksack as a blast of air nearly blew my jeans
off, and my feet lifted a couple of centimetres
from the ground! *Yikes!* I released the button,
landed awkwardly, and slipped the bag off in
panic, letting it fall to the ground. Underneath
the rucksack I could see two metal rims
protruding, like the ends of a couple of baked
bean cans. *Oh, wow!* They were mini jet thrusters;
Mamuk had given me a rucksack that could fly.
How brilliant is that?

I put the bag back on. *Right*, I thought; *if the
middle button is to turn the thrusters on, maybe the*

others are for direction. I tried again, gently pressing the middle button until this time I heard a soft click. Once again I took off and hovered about half a metre from the ground. Then I pressed the top button – and sure enough, I started to move forward. Pressing the middle button again, I rose up another couple of metres, going along at a steady jogging pace.

'This is brilliant!' I cried. 'This is— *Yikes!*'

Once, twice I flipped head over heels, right at the edge of the huge drop into the valley. I pressed the button a third time, and with the tiny thrusters humming like a swarm of mosquitoes, shot high into the air!

'No!' I yelled. 'Get me down from here!'

Why wasn't there an instruction book with this runaway rucksack? Closing my eyes and wishing hard, I pressed it once more. The thrusters subsided and I slowly started descending. Two more clicks and I was back on solid ground. Phew, that was scary. Scary, but fun! Perhaps the edge of a steep hillside wasn't the best place to practise; I would wait until I reached the valley floor and try again there.

Finding a narrow path that seemed to zigzag its way down towards the river, I marched along at a brisk pace. The sun was shining, the birds were twittering and the wide river twinkled in the distance. Everything was perfect; then, as I came round a bend in the path, *the world went black!*

'Hey, what's going on?' I yelled, and raising my hands, I felt some coarse material surrounding me. Someone had thrust a sack over my head. But who, and what for?

The world went black!

'Got him!' I heard a voice say. 'Let's take him down to the docks!'

'No!' I yelled in a real panic. 'Let me go! I'm supposed to be going to Jakeman's.'

'Well, you're not,' replied the voice. 'You're comin' with us, whether you like it or not.'

Help me

PUBLISHER'S NOTE
This is where Charlie's sixth journal ends. Who has captured him and what amazing adventures are in store for our intrepid explorer? Keep your eyes peeled for another incredible Charlie Small journal.

We'll get
you Charlie
Small
from the
brigands

Watch out, buster

Fantastic rocket powered rucksack

Is it a bird? Is it a Plane? No, it's Charlie Small — intrepid explorer!

The snow bazooka

loading hatch

Sights

Snow

sliding door

Trigger

Handle

Snowball — goes at 100 km per hour!

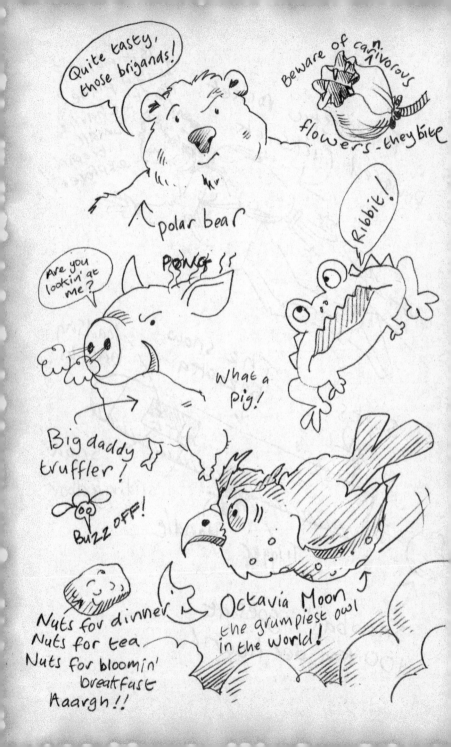